PENGUIN METRO READS
AFTER ALL THIS TIME

Nikita Singh is the bestselling author of ten novels, including *The Promise*, *After All This Time* and *Love@Facebook*. She has co-authored two books with Durjoy Dutta: *If It's Not Forever . . .* and *Someone Like You*. She has also contributed to the books in the Backbenchers series. Her latest novel, *Every Time It Rains,* was an instant bestseller. She was born in Patna and grew up in Indore. She graduated with a degree in pharmacy from Indore. Nikita has worked as an editor at Grapevine India for three years and as a publishing manager at Wisdom Tree before relocating to New York, where she got her master's in fine arts (in creative writing-fiction) at the New School. She received the India Young Achiever's Award in 2013 and has delivered TEDx talks at IIM Calcutta, IIM Indore, IIT Delhi, BITS Pilani and many other prestigious institutes. With a library stocked with over 12,000 books, she is a voracious reader and adores her collection of fantasy novels. She is currently based in New York.

After All This Time

Nikita Singh

Penguin
metro reads

An imprint of Penguin Random House

PENGUIN METRO READS

USA | Canada | UK | Ireland | Australia
New Zealand | India | South Africa | China | Singapore

Penguin Metro Reads is part of the Penguin Random House group of companies
whose addresses can be found at global.penguinrandomhouse.com

Published by Penguin Random House India Pvt. Ltd
4th Floor, Capital Tower 1, MG Road,
Gurugram 122 002, Haryana, India

Penguin
Random House
India

First published in Penguin Metro Reads by Penguin Books India 2015

ISBN 9780143424857

For sale in the Indian Subcontinent only

Typeset in Bembo by Manipal Digital Systems, Manipal
Printed at Repro India Limited

www.penguin.co.in

MIX
Paper from
responsible sources
FSC® C047271

This book is dedicated to all those who refuse to lose faith in love, despite the pain and horror and torment that accompany it.

Love takes off masks that we fear we cannot live without and know we cannot live within.

James Baldwin

Prologue

New Delhi, 2007

Lavanya clutched the books she was holding closer to her chest as she made her way through the school corridor. Maybe they wouldn't notice her if she walked by fast enough. But in her rush to escape, she stumbled on the stairs at the end of the hallway. She stretched out her arms to break her fall, scraping her palms in the process. Without caring to dust them off, she quickly knelt down to gather her books.

A boy approached her, and picked up the last book before she had a chance to. The rest of his group watched from close by.

'Need help?' the boy asked. He was in class twelve too, but in a different section. He had a square face, his tie was knotted loosely and the top three buttons of his shirt were undone. She had seen him around before but did not know his name.

'Thanks. Can I have that back?' Lavanya said nervously. She did not look at him, her eyes were fixed on the book in his hand.

'Don't wanna talk?'

'I have class.'

'*Science* class?' the boy sneered.

Lavanya could feel everybody's eyes on her. Her ears were becoming warm. She wanted nothing more than to run away. 'Can I have my book back, please?' she asked again, barely controlling her shaking voice.

'Why are you still stuck on that? What is this, the *science* book?' the boy chuckled, flipping the pages of the book.

Lavanya's lower lip was quivering. She did not want to humiliate herself further and give them the satisfaction of seeing her break down in front of everyone. 'Give it back to me,' she said fiercely, putting all her courage into that one sentence, and snatched the book from him.

There was hooting from his friends.

'What's going on here?' a stern voice asked from behind her. Three teachers were walking towards them, looking from her to the boy's group and then back at her.

'Mrs Dey! What a coincidence! We were just discussing science,' the boy said smiling, not intimidated in the least.

'Is everything okay, Lavanya?' Mrs Dey asked.

Lavanya nodded and rushed away.

1

New York, 2014

The sound of her five-inch heels clattering against the hardwood floors of the bright, fashionably decorated corridors of Paxton-Stark-Meester, one of the largest law firms in New York City, could be heard long before she came into view. But Lavanya Suryavanshi did not slow down to appreciate the minimalistic decor of the passageway; she had no time. She never did.

Lavanya readjusted the folder tucked under her left arm for the hundredth time. All the documents were in order. It was a big day at work. This was her chance to impress her direct supervisor; something she had been trying to do ever since she'd joined PSM, a little over a year ago. Every year PSM hired twenty new graduates from Harvard Law School as junior associates. When Lavanya had opened her mail and found that she had been invited to join the company, she could not believe her eyes. The screening process had been a rigorous, three-week affair that included written tests, group discussions and personal interviews. Thrilled, she rushed out of Starbucks with a steaming cup of coffee, and right into a man entering the coffee shop. Her cell phone slipped out of her hand and fell to the hard concrete floor.

'I'm so sorry! I totally didn't see you there,' she apologized, her mind whirling with the incredible news.

'Watch where you're going, lady!'

'My fingers slipped off the sleeve. They make the cups so hot—I'm sorry,' she repeated.

'Yeah, I know it's hot. You got it all over me!'

Another five minutes of public grovelling passed before the stranger grudgingly accepted her apology, and Lavanya finally patted herself down with the tissues a Starbucks employee was kind enough to hand her. She picked up her phone; the screen had shattered completely and no matter how many times she molested the power button, it refused to turn on.

'Perfect,' she muttered under her breath. Had she read the mail correctly or was she celebrating prematurely? Doubts plagued her as she rushed back to her apartment, politely refusing the server's offer for a replacement cup of coffee. It was only after she reached home and read the email again on her laptop half a dozen times that she allowed herself to relax. Maybe even smile.

Now, fourteen months later, she was still trying to make it into her supervisor Mr Cather's good books. Her first impression had been ruined when she arrived at the PSM office thirteen minutes late on the day of her orientation. When she explained how she got confused reading the subway map, Mr Cather's exact words had been, 'I hope for your sake that you read corporate law better than you read maps. We'd hate for a junior associate to leave us so soon.'

Ever since then, no matter what Lavanya did, she never could win points with Mr Cather. She was never assigned to any of the major cases, and was constantly saddled with mountains of paperwork, which meant she was inevitably the last one to leave the office. Irrespective of the late nights, she was always the first one to reach office the next morning, but of course, Mr Cather was never there to see that. And even if he did accidentally stumble to the office that early on occasion, he never had any reason to go all the way to the corner of the room where her cubicle was and see her immersed in work, an hour before the rest of the junior associates even checked in.

After fourteen months of being unimportant in the eyes of anyone consequential in the law firm, Lavanya had finally been given an opportunity to prove her worth to Mr Cather and hopefully the rest of her colleagues, who revelled in her humiliation. After all, it was easy for the nineteen of them to gang up against the one person who was already being picked on. Lavanya did not mind being the one who was repeatedly bullied by the rest of the junior associates. It gave her a reason to not hang out with them socially and make idle small talk. And though there were moments when she wished she had friends around, mostly she would much rather be left alone. 'It is the best way to be—you get more time to focus on your career and improve on your work.' Something—the *only* thing—she had been concentrating on for the past seven years.

Lavanya sighed again. She was ready for this. Everything she had done from the time she first started preparing for the law entrance examinations years ago had led to this very moment. This was her chance. She had everything in place— every single document double- and triple-checked, all of them arranged in the sequence she anticipated she would need them.

As she strode into the conference room now, she was relieved to see that Mr Cather was not yet in. She greeted Mrs Conklin and the opposing counsel briskly and took a seat across them, next to her client, Mr Bauer. Mrs Conklin was suing Mr Bauer for fraud and money laundering and although unfortunate for both of them, it was good news for Lavanya since it was the first major case she had been allowed to assist Mr Cather on. Or so she thought.

Fifteen minutes later, Joshua Saks, another junior associate, marched in through the glass door, huffing and puffing. He took the vacant seat next to Lavanya, the one Mr Cather was supposed to have occupied, and demanded to see her file.

'*What* do you think you are doing?' Lavanya hissed under her breath.

'Filling in for Cather. He's not going to make it,' Joshua responded, looking a little too pleased to be announcing this piece of news.

'What?! Why?'

'Oh, *I'm sorry*. When he called and asked me to take over, I didn't realize I was supposed to question his reasons.'

'What's with the attitude?' Lavanya responded heatedly.

'What's with the third degree?'

'This is not a joke; this is important. And you are also just a junior associate—'

'A junior associate who has been to a hundred such meetings in the past year. I've got it under control,' Joshua said with an air of finality and pulled the file out of Lavanya's hands. He turned to Mrs Conklin and the opposing counsel, 'Mr Cather sends his apologies that he won't be able to join us today. My name is Joshua Saks, I'll be filling in for him.'

And just like that, Lavanya's long-cherished fantasy of one day proving her mettle in front of Mr Cather was crushed yet again. She sat through the meeting with that ass Joshua instead of Mr Cather, feeling slighted, watching him say and do things that she had dreamt of saying and doing herself. She had to sit silently next to a colleague who was doing so for the hundred and first time, just because he had arrived at PSM thirteen minutes before she did.

The case was settled. Using her ideas and the laws she had read through and outlined to fit the case, Joshua convinced Mrs Conklin and her lawyer to drop the case in lieu of a settlement amount that was much smaller than what their client might have had to pay had the case gone to court. And as Joshua acted like a total rock star who basically lip-synced her songs, Lavanya sat quietly and stared at her lap, where chips of her fingernails were falling on her skirt as she assaulted them.

After the meeting was over, Lavanya nodded curtly at the others and watched them leave through the glass door, one by one. She stayed back. She had nowhere to go. For the past week, all her energies had been streamlined towards this meeting. She had been looking forward to presenting her ideas to the client in front of Mr Cather and dazzling him with her competence; not to having someone else snatch away her hard work and cakewalk through a meeting that had taken her a string of sleepless nights to prepare for.

She slumped back in her chair and sighed. Lavanya was constantly tired; not sleeping for more than five hours a night for seven years in a row would do that to anyone. Her head was bursting, but she could not even take her migraine meds for some relief, because she was going to a blood drive later in the afternoon and she could not have any drugs in her system.

Sometimes, on days like this, she would question what she was doing with her life. But not today. She was completely drained and had absolutely no energy left to reflect on her life choices and push herself further into depression. Instead, she just sighed once again, leaned forward, rested her forehead on the desk and closed her eyes.

~

Three minutes later, Mr Cather walked in and slapped the table Lavanya had fallen asleep on, jolting her awake in alarm.

'What do you think you're doing?' he bellowed.

'Huh?' Lavanya stood up hurriedly, her head spun, causing her to fall back in the chair, holding her head in both hands.

'Aww, did I wake Sleeping Beauty? I do hate to interrupt a fairy tale.'

'I am—I am so sorry . . .' Lavanya shook her head to try and make sense of the situation, but the motion just made her headache worse. She blurted out, 'I have a headache . . .'

'Get your shit together, Suryavanshi. I don't want to have to repeat myself. I've tolerated your sloppiness far too long. Have you gotten the message yet that I am not pleased?'

'Yes, Mr Cather . . .' Lavanya murmured. *On multiple occasions, for no apparent reason other than pure wickedness.* She sometimes wondered why he didn't just give up. Surely, some of the novelty of picking on her should have worn off by now, it had been going on for so long. She really was not a bad employee. In fact, trying to earn points with Mr Cather had driven her to push herself as hard as she could to be the best she could. Yet the way she was treated at PSM was downright spiteful.

'Good. Now, what happened with the Conklin meeting?'

'Mr Cather,' Joshua peeked into the conference room. 'I was just looking for you. The meeting went really well. We convinced them to settle.'

'Settle? You're joking!' Mr Cather's eyes lit up.

'I'm expecting the paperwork by the end of the day,' Joshua said, almost giddy with excitement, either on settling the case or impressing the boss, Lavanya neither knew nor cared enough to find out which.

'I have to say, that's some remarkable work, Joshua.'

Lavanya did not need to be a part of this. She got up, slowly this time, and walked towards the door after muttering a soft *Excuse me.* As she was about to exit the room, Joshua spoke up, 'Actually, Mr Cather, it wasn't just me. It was Lavanya's work. I used her notes and her arguments.'

'Where do you think you're going?' Mr Cather said, disregarding what Joshua had said.

'I'm . . . umm . . . to . . .' she mumbled. What just happened? Had *Joshua* just put in a good word about her to Cather? That was a first.

'Go grab your medical documents and get down to the blood drive. You know how important this client is for us. We need to show our support,' Mr Cather bit out.

'Uh . . . yes. That's where I was going,' Lavanya said.

Mr Cather shook his head and stepped out of the conference room. Joshua looked at her apologetically for a second and shrugged before following him out. So, finally, someone else had started pitying her situation. Awesome.

Lavanya rushed to her cubicle and gathered the test reports from her desk. Their client, one of the biggest healthcare centres in the country, had organized an all-day blood drive in the city. To show their support, the name partners at PSM had sent a circular throughout the offices, requesting all employees to volunteer.

Lavanya wondered if she could just hop in and out of the blood drive, quickly making her donation, and head home. She could not bear the idea of returning to work again, not that day. She needed rest.

She opened the envelope with her blood reports and quickly scanned through it. Just the basics: Suryavanshi, Lavanya . . . 10/10/1991 . . . O+ve . . . The rest of the medical jargon did not make much sense to her. She was about to fold the report and keep it back when her eyes caught something. She froze.

Forcing herself to stay calm, she scanned it again. The motion was mechanical; as if her eyes were following orders her brain was sending, without consciously realizing what she was doing. Her eyes focused on one particular section.

The world around her fell silent. She became strangely aware of all her body parts. She heard and felt the incessant thumping of her own heart. Her breathing became more laboured with every second. Her palms became clammy and her vision blurred until she could see nothing . . . nothing except . . .

HIV status: Positive

~

Shourya slipped into the apartment at 5 a.m., yawning widely. He took off his shoes, and picked them up, careful not to make any noise. Padding softly across the floor, he gently laid them down, and placed his books on the study table. He undressed himself in precise movements, not taking a second more than required. After gathering his clothes and throwing them in his laundry basket, he grabbed his towel, tiptoed out of his room and into the bathroom and bolted the door.

He breathed out. This was the tough part; no matter how hard he tried, the shower was going to make noise. His best bet was to block the spray with his body and make sure it did not touch the bathtub—that made the least amount of sound. He had plenty of experience; he had been doing this every morning for the last four months. He did not know if they couldn't hear him, or if they knew he was there and didn't come out of 'their' room while he was in the house out of courtesy. Or shame, hopefully.

A minute later, Shourya turned off the shower and dried himself. Wrapping the towel around his waist, he quietly unlocked the door and stepped out, intending to return to his room. Instead, he ran straight into *her*. His heart missed a beat.

Instantly, Shourya felt a dead weight at the pit of his stomach. He had not seen Deepti in three weeks. She had cat

eyes and lips so thin they sometimes disappeared completely
when she laughed. She was wearing a man's shirt—*his* shirt—
reaching mid-thigh, and her waist-length dark brown hair
cascaded down one shoulder in a bundled mess. She looked
like she had just woken up; her eyes were still sleepy, yet
somehow completely awake upon seeing him. She blinked
rapidly as if in confusion.

'Shourya?' she whispered.

'Yes, it's me. Don't look so shocked. I live here too,
remember, apart from your *other* boyfriend?' he muttered, gritting
his teeth and staring at the shirt she was wearing with disgust.

'That's not fair!' she said, her eyes downcast.

'Oh, *that*'s what's not fair?'

'Why are you being so mean? I thought we were over
this—' Deepti began, but Shourya cut her off.

'Stop it, Deepti; I'm not in the mood.'

'Mood for what? I'm not doing anything. You're the one
being mean.'

'Fine, then let me go to my room and we'll both forget we
bumped into each other just now,' Shourya said.

'But I don't want to forget. I want to know how you're
doing.'

'Never been happier. Can I go now?'

'You don't look very happy,' she said softly.

'*Not* born to please you, woman.'

'What is *wrong* with you—?' Deepti looked up at him, her
eyes wide like those of a hurt puppy.

'*Seriously?*' Shourya hissed, flipping his lid completely. The
words were out of his mouth before he could filter them. 'Are
you serious?' he bit out. '*Six years*, Deepti. Six years we were
together. I gave you everything I had and more. I did every
possible thing I could that I thought would make you happy.
And what did you do to me?'

'I've said I'm sorry—'

'And that makes it okay? That makes it okay for you to cheat on me, not once, not twice, but for months . . . *months* behind my back? And that too with one of my closest friends?'

'What was I supposed to do . . .? I fell in love . . .' Deepti started sobbing, like always. It was ridiculous how genuinely hurt she looked by his words.

'Stop it, Deepti. Seriously. Enough with the fake tears already. I still don't understand how you get to play the victim here. It's too early in the day for me to care about your bullshit. And the good news is that I no longer have any obligation to deal with it. So just, please . . .' He held up his hands, palms outward, and shrugged.

He shifted around her, expecting her to not prolong this encounter any more. But it did not seem like she had any intention of letting it go that easily. Just as he turned the knob of his bedroom door, she spoke again.

'Please don't be so rude to me, Shourya. You know what you mean to me. I never meant to hurt you. I really loved yo—'

That was the last straw. Shourya simply could not hold it together any longer. In a swift movement, he curled his fingers into a fist and punched the wall. The wood shattered, and his fist got lodged in the drywall behind it.

'Oh my God! What are you doing?' Deepti shrieked.

Shourya pulled his fist out angrily and shook it to relieve the pain.

'Don't you dare say that!' he roared. 'Don't ever say you loved me! If you want to tell yourself that so you'll feel like a less horrible person, so that you can sleep at night, fine! But do *not* say that to me. I've heard enough lies from you to last a lifetime. I don't want to hear any more.'

'What the hell is going on here?' Avik asked walking in, clearly woken up by the commotion.

'Nothing!' Shourya snapped. On seeing Avik's baffled expression, he added, 'Oh re*lax*, it's not like you walked in on your girlfriend making out with your friend, roomie. Trust me, that isn't the same.'

And with that, Shourya jerked open his bedroom door, walked in and slammed it shut. He had half a mind to go out there and confront them again. But the other half of him, the part that craved sanity, pulled him back. *How long was this going to go on? Would he ever be able to get out of the pit he had been pushed into?*

He recalled the first time he had seen Deepti. He had just joined college, and was still in the middle of picking and dropping classes, unable to decide which ones he wanted to keep, when he had seen her in the canteen. She was a fresher too, and his choices became easy—he simply picked the same classes she was taking. It took him quite some time to win her over. But when he finally did, after months of wooing, it was incredible.

They were inseparable throughout college. When they reached their final year, Shourya knew exactly what his next step would be: a business finance master's degree from Harvard Business School. It had been his dream ever since he had realized the direction he wanted to build his career in. Deepti, on the other hand, was still unsure about what she wanted to do after graduating. It was Shourya who convinced her to join him. She was neither as ambitious as him nor as bright a student, but Shourya was determined to go to the States, and he had no intention of leaving her behind and going alone.

All through their final year, Shourya coached Deepti and helped her study for the GRE while preparing himself. They spent every second of every day together, staying up till dawn on most nights, cramming, laughing over shared bowls of Maggi. Shourya would insist on having a tall glass of milk—his one obsessive regression to childhood—as they yawned their way through sunrise.

When they finally decided to call it a night, a few hours into the morning, they would lie down together on his single bed and hold each other as they dozed off. When they woke up a few hours later, they would go to their afternoon classes together. Deepti would head to her hostel afterwards, but would return to Shourya's again at night. And once more, they would stay up all night to study.

It became difficult to think of them as two separate beings. For most practical purposes, they weren't independent any more. They were strangely co-dependent, and Shourya felt that was truly the best way to be.

He had been happy.

When they started receiving admits from universities in the US, they were crushed to find out that Shourya had got into Harvard, but Deepti had not. It had been a long shot anyway; her chances had been slim, but they had still hoped. The only university that accepted both of them was the University of California, Berkeley, and even though Harvard was a much better option for Shourya, there was no way he was going there without her. Harvard and UCB were at the opposite ends of the US, and Shourya couldn't bear the idea of being 3000 miles away from Deepti for two years. They both knew that once school started, the coursework was going to take over their lives. The only way to stay together would be to study together.

When Shourya decided to enrol in UCB, Deepti did not dispute his decision. Not once did it occur to her that he was giving up something truly spectacular for her. She was twenty-one years old, going out of the country for the first time and scared out of her wits; she was much too grateful to have Shourya by her side to think of anything else.

Once they reached California, Deepti insisted they act as friends and not reveal their relationship to their classmates. She thought they would be alienated from the group and not considered individuals once everyone knew they were a couple. Shourya did not see any sense in the argument, but saw no reason to contest it either because he understood that she needed to do things her way to adjust to her new life in a foreign country.

Deepti got an apartment with two other girls and Shourya took another one, in the same building, with Avik. *Avik*. Just thinking about him now made Shourya's blood boil. He had considered him a good friend, not realizing that his girlfriend was developing feelings for his roommate. Shourya had first seen Deepti and Avik together in their final year of grad school, right before their end-of-term exams. He had come home from class, and when he pushed the elevator button to go up to his apartment, the doors opened to reveal Avik's arm around Deepti's waist. The way Deepti jerked Avik's hand away when she saw Shourya was enough to tell him what was going on.

She had confessed to him later. There had been a dirty scene where Avik claimed to have had no idea that Shourya and Deepti were in a relationship. Deepti had gone from having two boyfriends to none in a matter of minutes.

After graduating, Shourya had joined a firm, which sent him to train at Fremont for three months. The timing was perfect; Shourya had run away to Fremont, far from all the fucked-up-ness.

Unfortunately, once his training was over, he had to come back to the apartment he had shared with Avik. He had just started working and could not afford to move into a new place, so he was stuck in this nightmare. When he returned, Deepti and Avik were openly dating. He was not interested in finding out how that had happened, but Deepti claimed she was in love with Avik and he had forgiven her for lying to him. Shourya had tried to avoid them as much as he could, restricting his presence in the apartment, sneaking in and out before they got up and spending most nights crashing at the office or the library.

But his lucky streak had ended that morning. He had seen her after three weeks, and now he wanted to run away again. When his company had asked for his site preferences, he had chosen California, not because he had any special love for the state, but because he had too much there that he could not let go of. Maybe it was time he did. They were way too painful, these encounters.

He stared back at the door. He could hear the faint sounds of Deepti and Avik talking, a burst of laughter. Shourya's jaw hardened. He would ask his manager if the spot was still open at their Boston office.

It was time he moved out.

2

Lavanya blinked. *This can't be right. Something has to be wrong with this report. This simply cannot be right. There was no way.* But no matter how many times she denied it, the truth did not change. The proof was in her hand.

That concrete piece of evidence slipped from her fingers, swayed softly in the air-conditioned room for a moment before landing on the carpeted floor. It was swiftly followed by her own body as she sank to her knees. The carpet in her cubicle barely cushioned her fall, but the pain in her knees did not even register; her mind was suddenly swimming with memories of the past, *way* back in the past, a time that she had actively, completely shut out of her conscious mind, creating a barrier between her past and present.

So much for starting over.

That piece of paper took Lavanya back six years, when she had run off to Harvard Law School right after finishing school in Delhi, where she had spent the first eighteen years of her life. She had not looked back. Once in Massachusetts, she had drowned herself in her coursework and not come up for air until she graduated. And once that happened, she drowned herself again, this time in her job, working as a junior associate at Paxton-Stark-Meester.

Every second of every day she lived and breathed, she had thought only of ways to do her job better. She had been obsessed with proving her bullies wrong, of establishing her worth at PSM, her days and nights devoted to work, work and more work.

This can't be happening. This cannot *be happening.* The thought repeated itself over and over in her mind. She was too young. She felt like she had done nothing of consequence yet. She could not stop living in the middle of her life. It could not end that suddenly. Could it?

What did being HIV positive even mean? Did she have AIDS? Was she going to die? Her fingers started shaking violently, and her body suddenly felt very cold. Her breath was coming in gasps, and it felt like the earth was moving so fast that she couldn't even stand. Eventually, however, she managed to grab the edge of her desk and hoist herself up.

Get it together, she told herself. *You've been through worse.*

She took a deep breath. Wasn't someone from the hospital required to call her? It had to be protocol to deliver such news over the phone; sending the reports without a warning was just too cruel. Maybe they had called her; she needed to check her voicemail one of these days.

She did not know what to do next. The obvious first step was to go to a doctor and find out more. She would need to repeat tests, and also take specific diagnostic tests for HIV. It was only logical to get those tests done before meeting with a doctor to discuss her case. Or maybe she ought to look up on the Internet what being infected with HIV precisely meant. Though she doubted she would figure out much until she knew how badly she was infected, and to what stage the virus had spread. She was used to taking care of herself—mostly because there had been no one else to do that for her for a long time— and her brain automatically started working on a game plan.

But eventually it proved to be too much for her. She was too confused and clueless and scared to think rationally. She could not understand what she was feeling—there were so many thoughts racing through her mind at the same time. She felt like crying . . . and she never cried. She desperately wanted to talk to someone about it, but she had no one. A dead weight was stuck in Lavanya's throat. *This cannot be happening.* Moments after telling herself to get it together, she dissolved into full-blown panic. Her migraine was worse than ever; it felt like her head was going to explode. She did not know if she could handle it after all.

She rifled through the documents on her desk madly, trying to find a pen. When she finally found one, she reached for a notepad and her laptop. She keyed in 'hiv positive meaning' and opened the first few links. After reading halfway through them, she opened another tab and searched 'hiv and aids specialists in new york'. When the results came she pulled out her cell phone to dial the first phone number that popped up.

'What are you still doing here?' Mr Cather, of course, had taken that moment to stop by her cubicle.

Lavanya quickly exited her browser and closed the flap of her laptop. She did not turn around to face him. She never wanted anyone to catch her weak or vulnerable.

'I asked you a question, Suryavanshi.'

She took a few deep breaths, her chest heaving with fury. Maybe that was the emotion that decided to overtake all others at this time of extreme crisis. Maybe it was the distraction she needed. Anger was better than sadness, hopelessness, helplessness.

'Not now, Cather,' she said, spinning around in her chair and looking him in the eye.

'What?'

She just glared at him.

'*What* did you just say to me?' Cather asked even though it was clear he had heard what she had said and was furious about it.

'I said,' Lavanya said, very slowly and clearly, pausing at each word, 'not—now—*Cather.*'

'How dare you!' Cather thundered. 'How dare you speak to me like that! Do you know what I can do—?'

'Yes, I do! I do, you . . . you unethical, unforgiving, grudging, chronically resentful asshole,' she spat out every word with deliberation and distaste. 'I do. In fact, not just me, every junior associate in this office knows what you could do to me, and what you *have* been doing to me all this time. It's been over a *year.* You know how many days that is? How many nights? Nights I haven't slept, trying to do everything right, getting *every last detail* right, trying to not give you a reason to show me *exactly* what you could do to me?'

Cather just stared at her, obviously not having expected such an outburst from Lavanya, who, having begun at last, could not seem to stop. All the pent up emotion—the frustration, the anxiety, the terror she had faced, not just at PSM at the hands of Cather, but from when she first started preparing for her LSATs eight years ago—finally found an outlet.

'I have done everything I thought would make you happy, would make you see my work for what it is, not a biased perception of it. Would it kill you to be a normal human being? Seriously, just freaking act like a professional and do your job! Why the stupid power games and plots to insult me repeatedly?'

Cather finally found his voice. Nostrils flaring, he started, his anger making him stammer, 'Do you . . . do you have *any* idea . . . what you're saying . . . ?'

'Yes, I do,' Lavanya replied vehemently. 'I'm saying exactly what I should have said months ago. This has to stop.

You have to stop! You call yourself a mentor? You make us junior associates do all your work, and all you do is find new ways to make my life hell.'

'I—I don't know what you're talking about . . . you . . . insubordinate, disrespectful . . .'

'I respected you long enough without you ever having deserved it. Now I'm . . .' Lavanya paused, shaking her head in dejection. 'I'm . . . I'm done. I'm tired of this. I just . . . not any more.'

For a minute, it seemed like Cather was at a loss for words. People were peeking out of their cubicles to witness the commotion. But Lavanya saw nothing except Cather, her gaze piercing him. She kept shaking her head slowly from right to left.

'You are just a bully. You ruined my life,' she forced out through gritted teeth. 'This used to be my dream. This is what I always wanted to do . . . and you killed it. You killed my dream . . .'

To his credit, Cather did not say anything. It was the first time he, or anyone in the PSM offices, had seen Lavanya Suryavanshi so rattled. She had usually ignored all their jibes, not caring about anything anybody said or did to her. It was difficult to read Cather's expression. Other than the anger he was obviously feeling, his face also gave away confusion and . . . *Concern*?

Maybe he thought she would kill herself and he would be blamed. For one crazy second, she thought maybe she should—just to get back at him.

But Lavanya did not have the time or energy to sit and try to decipher Cather's moods and expressions any more. She grabbed her coat off the back of her chair, shoved her cell phone in her handbag and walked out of her cubicle, away from . . . everything.

When she walked out of the Paxton–Stark–Meester office, she knew she was never coming back.

~

For the next five days, Lavanya was a zombie. After reaching home, she had slept for sixteen hours straight. When she woke up, it was dawn. There was faint light outside, indicating that the sun was about to rise. She felt muddled, unsure of where she was, what she was doing there and how much time had passed. She had not slept for those many hours since . . . ever.

Lavanya was starving, but there was nothing to eat at home. All she found in her kitchen were some cups of flavoured yogurt that had expired, dry cereal and take-out menus. She decided to go out. She wore a long overcoat over her sweatpants and hoodie, zipped up her tall boots and wrapped a thick scarf around her ears and neck before stepping out. It was 1 December and as expected, it was freezing outside. Pulling her coat tightly around herself, she shivered as she walked, without any idea of where she was going.

From her apartment in West Village, she headed north on the vacant sidewalks, until she suddenly realized she was at Times Square. Having covered the two miles in a haze, she stopped only when she noticed the bright lights coming off the gigantic screens, brightening up the still-dark morning. The Square was always crowded, no matter the time of day or year. Lavanya saw a man wearing a round plastic head painted like a bald child's. He grinned at her, several teeth missing. It was December, in New York City—yet he wore nothing except a giant white diaper with a big fake safety pin on it and a pair of white booties. The things people did for money.

The thought struck Lavanya, and she stopped walking. She stared at him, her brows knitted in concentration as the man went from person to person, impersonating a baby, asking them if they wanted to have their picture taken with him, looking to get some money in exchange. And then she rushed to find the nearest ATM, took out cash and went back to the full-grown, almost-naked man-baby and gave him a hundred dollars. He grinned and insisted she take a picture with him on her phone. She did so, and walked on.

For the next five days, that was all she did—take cash out and give it to musicians at Subway stations, artists at Washington Square Park, dancers at Central Park and so on. She gave away a considerable chunk of her savings to fast chess players, painters at the streets, magicians and all sorts of other artists trying to earn some cash by performing for people. The one good thing about having drowned herself in work was that she'd never had a chance to spend any of her salary except on food, rent and her student loan instalments. She explored more of the city in those five days than she had done in the last sixteen months she had been living there.

By the fifth night though, Lavanya was exhausted. Her legs almost gave way because she had been walking so much. She decided to go home. She was scared, she was paranoid. She found it hard to understand the strange mix of emotions she was feeling. Was she so fatigued because of the miles and miles she had walked, or was it her disease?

Lavanya had completely ignored her test report after she first saw it. She hadn't been to a doctor, looked up anything on the Internet or called anyone for advice. She was hoping that if she did not think about it, it would eventually go away on its own. Of course, she realized that she was being delusional and needed to come out of it. But she was not ready to face the facts, not just yet.

First, she had to face something else—something she had been running from for too many years.

She picked up her phone and called a number she hadn't in a long time. It rang three times, and then, 'Hello?'

Lavanya paused for a short moment, and said, 'Mom? I'm coming home.'

~

Shourya finally managed to zip up his large suitcase, practically sitting on top of it to get it to close. As much as he adored his little sister, ordering him to bring twelve pairs of shoes from California to New Delhi was ridiculous, even bordering on mental abuse—he was going to kill Shreela. To her credit, she had made his job easier by sending him links of online stores and telling him what sizes and colours to get. All he had to do was go to the links, buy the insanely overpriced shoes, somehow shove them all into one large suitcase, add a few pieces of his own clothing, and he was packed for his trip to India.

He still could not believe Shreela was getting married. Even though she was only three years younger than him, their relationship was more like that of a parent and child. He had always treated her as his baby. When she had first told him about Manav, Shourya had been sceptical. But after the initial feeling of disbelief that his baby sister had grown up wore off, he had agreed to meet Manav. Eventually, it was he who had broken the news to their parents and convinced them that Manav and Shreela belonged with each other. After that, their families had met, decisions were made and now, finally, it was time for the big event. He had taken four weeks' leave from work so he could be at the wedding. To be honest, he did not really mind carting all those shoes for Shreela. She was his little sister, she was getting married, it was going to be the happiest day of her life—she could ask for his right arm and he would give it to her, gladly.

Shourya had called a cab service, and while he waited for it to arrive, he lay down on his bed and stared at the ceiling. The bumpy texture had always bothered Deepti. Maybe it wasn't as bad in Avik's room; he had never noticed. Never thought he would find himself looking up at the texture of his ceiling and comparing it to his roommate's to see what his ex-girlfriend thought of each of them. Her rejection did weird things to him. He found himself comparing himself to Avik all the time, as if it were a competition.

Ever since he had found out about Deepti and Avik, he had begun to look at Avik in a different light. Wondering what Deepti saw in him. Shourya and Avik were the same height, had gone to the same school, and lived in the same apartment. But Avik was a killer drummer. He had even been a part of the school band. There was an air of coolness about him, as if he didn't care for whatever was going on.

Shourya hadn't expected Avik to be as possessive of a girl as he was of Deepti. Maybe that was what Deepti liked about him. Perhaps Shourya had not been obsessive enough for her.

The cab arrived just then. In one swift motion, he got up and dragged his luggage out of the house. He was glad to be going away for a while. He desperately needed some time away from all of the messiness. Once in the cab, he sat back and closed his eyes. Maybe when he came back after his trip, things would be different. Maybe he would have forgotten some of the things he had been trying so hard to forget. Maybe he would be able to move on, to sleep at night. Maybe his hands wouldn't tremble every time he thought of the days and the nights he had spent with Deepti, of loving someone so deeply and so fiercely that he had felt handicapped by it. Maybe when he returned, his life would no longer be as fucked up.

3

Lavanya walked down the narrow aisle and out of the airplane. Her legs shook and she felt the sweat bead down her spine, making her top stick to her back. She felt strangely cold and hot at the same time. While waiting to collect her luggage, she had half a mind to run back to New York. She undid her messy high bun and let her hair fall around her face, hiding as much of her pain as she could.

It was very early in the morning in India, but Lavanya was already feeling sleepy, thanks to the jet lag. Once she got her bags and heaved them on to a trolley, she decided to get a coffee. She convinced herself that she was not trying to delay meeting her parents, and that she really did need caffeine in her system in order to function.

But no matter how long she wandered around the airport, she could not put off leaving it indefinitely. She felt like she had nowhere else to go. After years, she had wanted to come home—the apartments she had rented over the years in a foreign country had never felt like home to her. She supposed she could go back, but she did not know what she would do there any more. It felt like she had nothing left there to go back to. She had practically destroyed her future at PSM, so her career, the one thing she had cared about, was lying on the floor in pieces. Besides, who in their right mind would go to an office to work for someone else and help them grow and make money when their days were numbered?

Get it together. She finally pushed her luggage cart out through the gate, slowly but determinedly, and looked around. It was not hard to spot them. Her mother was smiling widely and waving at her in glee. When Lavanya waved back hesitantly, her mother covered her mouth with her hand, the crinkles around her eyes turning slightly downwards, just like her lips, Lavanya imagined, under the hand hiding them. Lavanya did not look at her father's face, but she could see that he was standing right next to her mother, his arm resting lightly around her shoulder. She noticed the arm.

She pushed her cart around the barriers and reached them. Her mother had almost broken down by then. She shrieked, 'Lavi!' and rushed towards Lavanya, pulling her into a tight hug. Lavanya hugged her back, and could feel the sobs shake her mother's body, so she just held her tighter. She had no words, and she herself was fretting about meeting her father.

'Mom,' Lavanya whispered.

'It has been so long since I saw you . . .' her mother sobbed. 'My child.'

'How have you been?'

Her mother did not respond to the question. Instead, she peppered Lavanya's cheeks and forehead with kisses, holding her as if scared that she would run away again.

It's okay, Mom, I'm here now. The words were at the tip of Lavanya's tongue, but she could not bring herself to say them. She was not going to be there for long . . . not even if she wanted to. Hiding the truth was one thing, but she did not want to lie to her mother. She stayed in the embrace for some time, because she was stalling having to greet her father, because her mother needed it and because no one had hugged her for more than three seconds in the past six years.

When her mother let her go at last, Lavanya took one step, just one step, towards her father. Placing an arm around his narrow waist, she leaned into him somewhat, and stayed there, half-hugging him for one second, before pulling back. She congratulated herself for managing that feat.

'It's good to see you,' he murmured. She had not heard the deep baritone of his voice since she had left Delhi. She had called her mom occasionally to check up on her and how things were, but never once spoken to her father.

Lavanya nodded.

In the car, an awkward silence settled over them and no one spoke for the first five minutes. Lavanya sat in the rear seat so she would not have to be close to her father, who was driving. She looked out of the window, at the city, *her home*. This was the only place that she had ever called home, that had ever felt like home. The honking cars, two-wheelers trying to overtake everyone else, that too, from the wrong side, pedestrians crossing the streets haphazardly, with speeding vehicles driving right at them, screeching to a stop just millimetres from them. Nearly everyone was abusing everyone else. It was chaos.

New York had been a different kind of chaos. It had been organized—even though there were pedestrians everywhere, not waiting for the walk sign to tell them it was safe to cross roads, cabbies driving like mad men, newspaper stalls and halal carts on every street. But it was still quiet. There was a rush, but it was a silent rush; it showed in the way people walked—swiftly, taking big steps, single-mindedly heading towards their destination. People rarely bumped into each other on sidewalks, so there were no *excuse me*s or *I'm so sorry*s; they all knew where they were going, they were all used to the pace.

Here, in India, especially in Delhi, it was a contrast. It was loud. The first five minutes after Lavanya got on the road drove her crazy. So much honking. People were in a rush, yes, but only half of them. The other half was walking or driving leisurely as if taking a stroll through the park. There were abuses flying around. Ah. What a pleasure to get home to expletives in your mother tongue.

Once they crossed the Delhi Cantonment area, a place much quieter than most parts of Delhi, they found a roadblock ahead. Some politician was on tour, leaving behind traffic havoc in his wake. The hustle-bustle of the residential-cum-commercial neighbourhood, Karol Bagh, cheered Lavanya up. As they rounded a corner, they reached the Hanuman temple, with a 108-feet tall statue of the god standing proudly, watching over the city. His hands were folded at his chest, and between his feet lay the head of a demon he had defeated. Lavanya had passed that temple hundreds of times, drawing strength every time.

The silence in the car was killing her. Lavanya rolled down her window, feeling the morning sun on her face, mixed with the cool air. She closed her eyes for a minute and breathed in—it smelled of leaves and concrete, and dust and petroleum oil. She had missed the city. There was no place like New Delhi. She tied her hair back and stuck her head out of the window for a while longer until she started finding it difficult to breathe. She closed the window and rested her head back. Just when she began contemplating jumping out of the car, to escape the silence, her mom spoke up.

'Really cold here, isn't it?'

The one thing people talk about when they have nothing left to talk about—the weather. *It has come to this.* All Lavanya said was, 'Yeah, it is quite cold.'

'Though you are coming from New York, so this must not feel that cold to you.'

'That's true.'

'Is it really cold there now?' her mom turned back and asked.

Lavanya thought back to the last week that she had spent walking around the city in the dead of the night, laden with overcoats and thick scarves wrapped around her neck. She had always ended up feeling hot and sweaty inside all the winter wear from walking so much. 'Yes, it was really cold there.'

Her mom nodded and turned halfway. She sat like that for a few moments, facing neither backwards nor ahead, maybe trying to think of something to say next, and then she turned forward, as if unable to think of anything.

The silence enveloped them all once again. It had been too long since they had been around each other. Too long since they had shared each other's company, spoken to each other, lived with each other . . . loved each other. They had forgotten how to simply *be* in each other's presence.

They had forgotten how to be a family.

~

Seeing her family home as her father drove in through the front gate shocked Lavanya. She somehow remembered it being much bigger than it was. Perhaps she had reconstructed her memories to make them greater, grander, more magical than the truth. But she did not feel that she had lived away from home long enough to have a warped memory of it, nor had she been so young when she left to have imagined it to be something it was not.

When she walked into the hall, all she could relate to was its basic structure, the shape and the general area. She remembered tall pillars and the chandelier, but everything else was new to her—the colour and texture of the walls, the tiny lights on the ceiling, the curtains, the vases, the centre table. She did not recognize any of that. Too much had changed.

The threadbare brown sofa with elephants embroidered on it was missing, and had been replaced with what looked like a plush leather couch. The carpet, though, was the same that she had seen the last time she was home.

As she went further inside, to the kitchen, the hallway, the bedrooms, she could swear they had been bigger back then. Somehow they had all grown smaller, over time, as if shrinking with age. Yet somehow, they seemed *younger*, more beautiful than ever. Lavanya was fascinated.

She had not expected to feel happy on coming home. She had wanted to come here just as an escape from her 'real' life. But when she stepped inside her room, she actually smiled. The slight movement of those muscles felt almost alien to her face.

'Lavi! Are you hungry? What do you want to eat?' her mother called from the kitchen.

Lavanya came back downstairs, only then realizing that she was starving; it was dinner time in New York. 'What do we have?'

Noticing the first glimmer of genuine interest in Lavanya, her mom felt relieved and somewhat excited. 'Let's see—I've made bhaji, I can heat up some pavs—'

'Say no more, Mother!' Lavanya raised her hand dramatically.

Her mom laughed. 'But I have also made chhole and samosas for you!'

'I told you it was going to be a waste of time. You did not need to make anything else. Lavi loves pav-bhaji,' her father interjected good-naturedly.

'I know—you were right. You know your daughter very well—'

'I will also have a samosa,' Lavanya said quickly, cutting her mom off once again.

It was followed by a brief silence.

'I'll heat one up for you. I wanted to cook all of your favourite dishes. God knows what you have been eating over there. You have come back after so many years . . .'

'I have been eating healthy, Mom. You don't have to worry.'

'What healthy! Look at you! You're all bones, you've lost so much weight.'

'I was always like this,' Lavanya muttered. What were moms without their you-have-become-so-thin dialogues?

'She was. She has always been skinny,' her father said.

'But she was a teenager then, now she is a grown woman!' her mom said and then added softly, 'God, it has been too many years.'

Lavanya decided to concentrate on all the yummy food on the table in front of her. The guilt for staying away could wait. When her mom served the first piece of warm pav and Lavanya took the first bite of the spicy and buttery bhaji, she forgot all her reasons for having left home. Her mom was an excellent cook. Lavanya knew everyone thought that about their mom, but her mother actually was the best cook in the world. She enjoyed cooking so much, and prepared everything with so much love and effort, paying attention to every last detail, that her food was never any less than the best.

Lavanya ate like she had not eaten in weeks, relishing every bite. 'This is so delicious, Mom!' she exclaimed between bites.

Her mother's face lit up with a warm glow, as if from within. She liked nothing more than feeding her family. Cooking was her way of showing love. She rarely indulged in physical displays of affection. 'Do you want some more? Take another samosa.' Before Lavanya could say anything, she had placed one on her plate.

'I'm full till here, Mom!' Lavanya protested, pointing to her neck.

'You've become too thin, Lavi. I don't like this.'

So Lavanya ate, and ate some more till her mom was satisfied. Her father did not say anything else throughout breakfast; he ate in silence.

'Mom, you're barely eating yourself. And you have lost weight too! You need food more than I do!' Lavanya said, only then noticing how thin her mother had become. Her face was no longer round; her cheekbones were more prominent now.

'Oh, I needed to. I did not want to stay a fat woman always!' her mom retorted.

'You weren't fat!' Lavanya and her father said together.

They looked at each other in reflex, but Lavanya quickly glanced away. When she looked down at her plate, she did not see what was on it. What she saw instead was the grey in her father's sideburns, the once black-and-white stubble that was now almost completely white, his thin lips that closed together to form a straight line, the expression on his face when he looked at her.

'Oh, I was. We all know that,' her mom said, not noticing anything amiss.

'No, you weren't,' Lavanya said, waiting for a second before speaking.

Shortly after, she went upstairs to her bedroom with her mom, who showed her where everything was, while Lavanya stood by, feeling like a guest in her own home. But she did not have the energy to care. Her eyelids were barely staying open. She yawned loudly as she climbed under her comforter and her mom closed the curtains.

'Good night,' Lavanya muttered as her head touched the pillow. 'Or morning, whatever.'

'Sweet dreams, Lavi. We missed you,' her mom whispered before stepping out of the room and quietly closing the door behind her.

Lavanya opened her drooping eyelids for a second, and let them roam around the room. She breathed in the smell and ran her fingers over the bed sheet. Things were not the same, but still somehow similar. She could hear her mother clearing the dishes off the table downstairs while her father spoke to her in a low tone, but she could not hear what they were saying. So far, she had mixed feelings about returning home. But it had certainly not been bad. Not bad at all.

In fact, it felt really good to be home.

~

Shourya reclined on the couch, exhausted. Getting the two women he loved the most in the world on the same page was an impossible task. His sister wanted a small wedding, and did not see why they had to invite long-lost relatives from far away and forgotten acquaintances of their parents she had never even met. Her reasoning made sense, but his mother was of the opinion that not having a grand wedding for their only daughter would be an insult to their reputation.

Shreela, all five-feet-two-inches of her, with her cute, angular face and little nose, which flared when she was angry, like it was doing now, was trying her best to remain calm and somehow convince her mother to let her decide the guest list. Her cheeks were pink and she looked like she was barely controlling herself from pulling her own hair out.

Their mother, on the other hand, seemed perfectly at peace as she presented her reasoning to her children. After all, she had raised Shreela—that would teach anyone patience, and compared to the time Shreela was a teenager, this was a piece of cake. Nevertheless, it was quite challenging to reason with the little packet of rebellion, short temper and stubbornness to boot.

'Bhaiya, help me. You explain to her. She always listens to you!' Shreela turned to Shourya, yet again, her eyebrows furrowed in frustration, as if this was the most important conversation of her life where she was being denied the only thing she'd ever wanted. Knowing her well he knew that as soon as this matter was resolved, something else would become equally critical.

'I'm not getting involved.' Shourya put his hands up, palms out, in surrender.

'But why!'

'Because the both of you are imposs—' he stopped himself just in time. Not the right time to start another argument. 'I'm just not getting caught in the middle of the two of you.'

'This is so unfair. This is *my* wedding. I should get to choose who should be invited and who shouldn't!'

'You are our only daughter. This is our only chance to throw a grand wedding. What will people think of us if there are only two hundred people there?' Mrs Kapoor said.

Shourya looked at his mother. She looked hassled and careworn. Her hair was messy, strands had escaped from the thick braid she always wore it in, and her square, wire-rimmed spectacles rode low on her nose. She only needed them to read, but she always forgot to take them off afterwards, so when she spoke she would pull her chin in and look at people from above the rims. It made her seem older than she was, like an old schoolteacher in fact. Shourya found that endearing.

'I don't care about a large audience! This is not a circus. It's my wedding. I want a small, private event, where I don't have to meet and be introduced to seven hundred people I've never met before and will never meet again. It's just torture!'

'You'll have to meet them for just a second—your dad and I will take care of them for the remainder of the night!'

'This is my only wedding!'

'This is our only daughter's wedding too! Think about all the gifts you're going to get!'

'I don't care about the stupid gifts! How many sets of china and photo frames and lamps and light bulbs and wall clocks do I need?'

'Don't be silly, no one is going to gift you light bulbs.'

'Mo-*om*.'

As much as he had tried to stay out of this one, Shourya knew he needed to intervene when he heard his sister drag out 'mom' the way she did. It was a sign that her frustration and her patience had reached a critical low. It was time for him to step in.

'What if, instead of having a super private or a super grand wedding, we have an average-sized wedding? We invite only people all members of our family know, so we don't offend someone who is important to any one of us by not inviting them,' he said, looking at his mom, and then turned to his sister, 'and Shreela, you won't have to meet absolute strangers. A compromise.'

Shreela looked at him as if he had gone crazy. Eyes narrow, mouth open in amazement, not saying anything, as if speechless at the silliness of what he had just proposed.

'What? It's a win–win situation!' Shourya defended himself.

'No, if we do that, *nobody* wins. It's a lose–lose situation.'

'It's not about winning or losing.'

'But you just said it's a win–win situation.'

'Okay, fine. Then let Mom win this one.'

'Did I do something to you?'

'All I'm saying is that if it really means that much to Mom, don't you think you can smile at a few extra people at the wedding?'

'No!'

'Wow! So considerate.'

'Shut up!'

'Polite too.'

'Bhaiya, please no!'

'Manav's parents are going to have hundreds of guests unknown to you anyway. What's a few hundred more?' Shourya asked. 'It is unfair, if you ask me—that you'll let Manav's parents invite all these strangers and not show the same love to your own mother.'

'I'm getting married into that family, so I will have to meet and get to know the people they know anyway,' she argued.

'Oh, yeah? Do you think Manav knows all of them?'

'I . . .' Shreela started, in the same rushed, indignant, high-pitched tone she had used in the entire conversation, but then paused, as if thinking about it for the first time. 'I don't know.' She sighed.

'Of course he doesn't! They're his parents' guests. His parents are allowed unlimited guests, then why doesn't Mom get to invite the people she wants?'

Shreela hesitated for a moment, shying away from her brother's eyes. He knew he had finally won this. Of course it was about winning or losing.

'Yeah?' he prodded.

All of a sudden, Shreela burst out, 'But you don't get it— it's not like that! I can't *do* anything about them! They are my in-laws!'

'And this is your own *mother*. Your own *blood*. The woman who kept you in her belly for nine long months. You can't let her invite her friends to her *only* daughter's wedding for a few hours?' Shourya shook his head repeatedly, lips pursed. 'Never expected this from you. You disappoint me.'

'Don't say that!' Shreela cried. 'Fine! Mom, you can have your guests. Fine.'

Shourya's lips stretched in a small smile; he chewed on the inside of his cheek to stop it from spreading. He looked at Shreela, her almond eyes shining with unshed tears, her face red, her lips trembling, and saw that she was biting her lower lip to keep from breaking down. He loved his sister; she was a brat most of the time, but he did love her.

Mrs Kapoor looked from her one child to another, unsure of what to say. Finally, she walked up to Shreela, kissed her lightly on the forehead, and said, 'Thank you.'

Shourya could barely hide the laughter bubbling inside him. 'Come here,' he said softly.

Shreela got up from her bean bag and walked towards him reluctantly, still not looking at him.

He got up and pulled her into his chest.

She hugged him back, burrowing her head under his chin.

'You're too cute, you know that?'

'But I disappoint you.'

'Aw, man. Was that all I needed to say to get you to agree? I could've saved myself the fight had I known that!'

'That was mean! Such a mean thing to say.'

Shourya bent and kissed his kid sister on the top of her head. Then ruffled her hair with his fingers, making her madder at him.

~

He was ashamed. At least that's what Shourya told himself as he lay on his bed that night, sleep still miles away from his eyes. But he was not convinced, he never was any more. He knew he was lying. He had known he was going to do it, he had done it, and no matter how much he cursed and loathed himself for it now, he knew he was going to do it again. Soon probably, depending on how long it took for his ego to crash and fall at the floor.

He would call her again.

When he was around his family and friends all day, he fooled himself into believing that he was okay. Yet he was lying, cheating, betraying and breaking all the promises he'd made to himself, repeatedly. Every time he thought about her, he resolved to stop. Each time he called her, he swore it was the last time. Every night when he went to sleep, he vowed the next morning would be a new beginning. But when morning came, he would wake up, expecting to see her beside him.

The most confusing part of all this for him was that he never really thought of the good times they had spent together, or missed the years of happiness. Whenever he thought of Deepti now, he thought of how it had ended, of what she had done and how it had affected him, changed who he was. And no matter how hard he tried, he knew he could never go back to being the person he was before his love and devotion were paid back for with betrayal and disloyalty. His heartbreak had him doubting that he could ever become whole again.

After finishing the day's shopping, when they had returned at 11 p.m., Shourya was exhausted. He had hoped he would fall asleep as soon as he lay down, but when, even after an hour, he found himself lying on his side and staring at the ancient wooden cupboard in the corner of his childhood room, he realized he was not going to sleep any time soon. And that he was going to call her again.

One thing happened differently though; this time, Deepti answered. And that's when matters got out of hand. Giving into temptation and calling one's ex in a moment's weakness is one thing—it shows the ex that you're sad and pathetic and are still thinking about them, that you still haven't moved on and built a new life for yourself since they've been gone. But if the ex does take the call, and is listening—oh, that's when shit really hits the fan—that's when instead of their just assuming all those things about you, *you* prove all their assumptions right, which is a thousand times worse.

He was thrown at first, hearing her real voice; he usually got her voicemail. And then he did not know what to feel, what to say, how to talk to the girl he had planned on spending the rest of his life with. He was not angry, not much, that night. He was confused, he was lost, and he was sad. Mostly sad. He missed her, and for once, he did not have the energy to hide his vulnerability and anguish behind the veil of anger or annoyance.

'Hello . . .?' she said for the fifth time as he pulled himself together.

'Deepti . . .' he said.

'Shourya? Yes, this is me.'

'How are you?' he asked softly, hoping she was doing as horribly as he was.

'I'm okay . . .'

Shourya nodded, pursing his lips.

'How are you, Shourya?'

'What do you care?'

'I do care. You know that.'

'You keep saying that. But I don't.'

'You do.'

'I really don't.'

Deepti sighed loudly. 'Please let's not do this, Shourya. I'm tired too. I care about you, and you know that. I want to know how you are doing.'

He was silent for a minute. 'I'm not fine.'

'Why not? I want you to be fine.'

'Maybe you don't always get want you want, after all?'

'Shourya.'

'You wanted me, and then you wanted him and didn't want me any more, so you left me.'

'I did not leave you.'

'Yeah, right. You didn't leave me. You simply started dating him too, behind my back, behind his back.'

'He knows everything about me.'

'Everything you have told him.'

'I've told him everything.'

'Like you told me everything?'

'Shourya.'

'Saying my name does not change anything.'

'Fine! I lied to you. I accepted that. I have apologized to you for it so many times. We did not tell anyone about us, no one knew we had been dating for four years when we came here, including him. So it was not his fault; he had no idea I was with you when I fell in love with him. Please don't feel like he betrayed your trust. You mean a lot to him. You were his best friend. It was my fault, I know that. I know I ruined everything. But it has been so long now. We know everything. We've all moved on. Can't we just forget about it already?'

Shourya shook his head slowly, repeatedly, his cell phone stuck to his cheek. He was amazed at how neatly Deepti had summed up the situation, as if there wasn't a storm rising inside of him every time he remembered that she belonged to someone else. All he did was shake his head. He did not trust himself to speak. He would simply remind her of all she had put him through, and he knew how pitiable it would sound. For once, inflicting pain on her to make himself feel better held no appeal.

He really did miss her.

So he let her speak, and just listened as she tried, and failed, to make him feel better, as she broke down several times, trying to explain, to justify everything. At one point, he almost bought into it; he almost felt as if she had been the helpless, clueless victim in the situation, that she still loved him and cared for him as much as she had before. Just not more than she loved and cared for Avik, of course not. The way she put it, it felt as if she really did not understand his point of view. Listening to her side of the story, Shourya felt like she was talking about somebody else, so different had the experience been for each of them.

For the next hour, she spoke mostly and he listened. He thought he felt better than he had before he had called her; that's how he justified the phone call to himself. He was not going to deny himself that relief just because reaching out to the person who ripped you apart to help put you back together was a pitiable thing to do.

But just when he thought he was arriving at a better place, he heard Avik's voice in the background.

'Why are you crying? What's wrong?' Avik was asking.

Shourya heard Deepti mumble, 'I'm okay, it's nothing,' before Avik took the phone from her.

'Hello? Who's this?'

'It's Shourya. Hey.' It was twisted. It was complicated. But it was how it was, how it was going to remain. Avik really was not to blame for any of this anyway. Maybe Shourya was finally ready to let go and move on.

'Shourya! I knew it. I knew it was you. Why do you keep calling her? This has been going on too long. Why won't you just leave us alone? Look at her—she's crying. Stop torturing her, man!' Avik barked.

'I did not do anything.' Shourya ground his teeth together, suddenly furious too.

'It doesn't seem like it. She's mine, okay? She decided that months ago. I take care of her now. You need to get the hell out of our lives and get one of your own.'

'Avik!' Shourya heard Deepti cry out.

'She can decide whether she wants to talk to me or not. You don't *own* her,' Shourya snapped.

'But I do have a say in what she does and doesn't do. And I'm telling you—stop bothering my girl. She has been through enough al—'

'Shourya,' Deepti shouted, 'don't listen to Avik. He's just upset because I was crying—'

'Damn right I am. Why do you have to talk to him—?'

'He's my best friend—'

'No, he isn't. He *was* your best friend, *and* your boyfriend, once upon a time, but isn't any more. Or have you forgotten that?'

'I didn't mean—'

'Of course you didn't mean it! You do nothing; things just happen around you.'

'Avik, please—' Shourya heard Deepti plead.

'Tell me, Deepti, do you still love him?'

'No, I don't! I've told you a million times—'

'You made your choice. You swore to me that you don't love him any more—' Avik said angrily.

'And I don't! I don't love him. I told you, I fell out of love with him a long time ago, I was just . . . I was stuck with him. I didn't know how to tell him . . . we'd been together for such a long time . . . I didn't want to hurt him.'

'But you did. It had to happen, and it happened. It was a long time ago. Then why are we still here—talking about this?'

'It's not that easy. There's so much history . . . it's so complicated . . .' Deepti cried.

'It's complicated only because you make it complicated. I've told you a hundred times to put him in the past. Just forget about him already, damn it!'

'I have! He means nothing to me. I love you . . . Avik, listen to me, look at me—I love you. Only you. You know that. No one else matters to me any more . . .'

Shourya pulled the phone away from his ear, and disconnected the call.

I fell out of love with him a long time ago.

I was stuck with him.

He means nothing to me.

4

Denial requires a lot of work. Your brain has to actively keep you away from something, every minute of every day. That takes work.

The mornings were long. Lavanya found herself wide awake before 4 a.m. almost every day since she'd come home. By the time her parents woke up and started their day, she had already spent hours thinking and worrying about what she was trying so hard not to think and worry about, and getting her head twisted in a knot—one she then tried to untangle all day. Being around her father only made matters worse. So she made an excuse of needing fruit juices and fat-free milk and what not to get out of the house.

'Mom, I'll be okay, really!' Lavanya said for the fourth time. 'It's just five minutes away, I think I can handle driving there on my own.'

'But I can drive you there. It really is no trouble.'

'No, Mom, you have to take care of Dad's breakfast before he leaves for work. Go back inside, he must be getting late.'

Mrs Suryavanshi looked at Lavanya and then back towards the house. 'Okay, be safe. You know how people drive around here,' she said and rushed back inside.

'I do.'

But it turned out she really did not. She had been a teenager, not eligible to drive, back when she lived in Delhi. She had occasionally 'borrowed' her parents' cars for midnight escapades, but never regularly. And driving in the States did not prepare her for driving in India, not even close. To begin with, she had to drive on the left side (which was a big adjustment), there were a hell lot more vehicles on the roads, no one seemed to care about lanes, people were overtaking her from either sides, no one giving a damn about pedestrians, and unless it was a main road with traffic signals people were basically driving without laws and regulations.

'What the . . .! Seriously?' Lavanya muttered, as a guy on a bike cut into her lane and braked suddenly. She stopped just in time to avoid a crash. She rolled down her window, stuck her head out and hollered, 'Hey!'

The rider ignored her; he was too busy fishing out his cell phone from his pocket—large phones and tight pants don't go well together. Having squeezed it out, he fixed it in his helmet somehow and rode away.

Lavanya sighed loudly and started the car again. It took her half an hour to cover the five-minute distance. Between keeping an eye out for wayward drivers and pedestrians, and remembering that she was now driving on the opposite side of the road, she briefly considered abandoning the car and walking back home to fetch her mother. But she knew she would never hear the end of it.

When she eventually parked outside the grocery supermarket, she knew it wasn't worth the effort she had put in getting there. But she was there, so she went in. She picked up a box of corn flakes and compared it to another box. The one with strawberries promised eight essential vitamins and iron power. But then again, there was another box of cereal that had chunks of chocolate in it. Since Lavanya was in no rush to go home she started reading from the back of the second box, leisurely, like it was the most interesting piece of literature in the world.

'Lavanya Suryavanshi?'

She spun around at the sound of her name.

The first thing she noticed was the hair. Oh God, so much hair. Long strands of thick black hair that fell to his shoulders in waves and framed a thin, angular face. It was everywhere—on his forehead, covering his ears and even his eyes somewhat. Then she noticed the beard, which, as if in contrast with his hair, was light, and scattered, more like a stubble really.

Apart from these two glaring changes, he was the same. Exactly the same. The same deep-set dark brown eyes under mismatched eyebrows (one slightly lower than the other, and more pointed towards the tip), the same straight nose (slightly nicked at the base, the result of a childhood injury), the same almost perfectly square jaw, lips that formed deep creases around his face and revealed a set of straight teeth when he smiled, like he was doing then.

'Shourya Kapoor!' Lavanya exclaimed. 'I *cannot* believe it's you! What are you doing here?'

Shourya pulled her into his chest and hugged her tightly, his arms wrapped around her as he rocked her from side to side, the way he always used to do. 'God, how many years has it been?' he pulled away and held her at an arm's distance to examine her.

'*Years*,' she said, looking up at him.

'Like a decade?'

'No, not a decade. Trust you to exaggerate facts.'

'Three years short of a decade; it's not that much of a difference. Trust you to undermine facts.'

'I—'

Before she could say anything else, Shourya pulled her back into another hug. He was six-feet tall, towering a good eight inches over her. So when he hugged her, her face burrowed into his chest. He smelled of cologne and mint and man, strong and warm and somehow still familiar after all these years.

She looked up at him. 'What are you doing here? And where have you been?'

'Where have *I* been? Where have *you* been? You completely disappeared. There's no trace of you on social networks!'

'Are you seriously lecturing me right now for not being active on Facebook?' Lavanya rolled her eyes. 'We are meeting after such a long time, and of all the things we could talk about you are choosing to criticize my social media presence, or absence or whatever!'

Shourya grinned. 'No, but at least show your face sometimes, so people can know what's going on in your life.'

'It's all very by-the-book and dull. You'll get bored.'

'You could never bore me, Lavanya Suryavanshi.'

'In that case, why didn't you call some time to ask what was going on in my life?'

'Hey! I did. Several times, but you were always caught up with one assignment or the other. You wouldn't take my calls, wouldn't respond to my texts. Not that I'm blaming you or anything . . . but eventually, I had to give up.'

'So that's what not blaming me sounds like!' Lavanya raised an eyebrow.

'Come on! I'm not. The time difference! *That's* the real culprit,' he winked.

'Uh-huh. And what about when you came to the States? Then the time difference was only three hours. You could have called me then.'

'Now who's blaming whom?' he narrowed his eyes.

'Okay, okay!' Lavanya held up her fingers in a sign of peace. 'What are you doing here?'

'I'm here for Shreela's wedding. We went to your place—Mom wanted to invite your parents in person. Your mom told me you were here, so I decided to follow you.'

'Shreela is getting married?' Lavanya exclaimed. 'To whom? How did they meet? Is it a love marriage? What does the guy do? How did this happen? When's the wedding? Tell me everything!'

'I will, I will! Slow down, woman! Didn't know you were such a fan of weddings.' Shourya laughed. 'But do you really think a grocery store aisle is the best place to catch up?'

'Oh, right.' Lavanya smiled and looked around sheepishly. For a moment, she had forgotten where she was, what had brought her there and all the other sad details of her life.

'We have to catch up properly. What are you doing here anyway?'

'I just . . . needed a break . . . and it was the holiday season, so I flew home.' She did not look at him. He could always sense when she was lying.

'No, I meant *here*, the grocery store?'

'Oh, nothing. I thought I'd go for a drive.'

'Thought?' he raised one of his eyebrows and smirked at her.

'What, I didn't realize it would be so hard to drive on these roads after so many years! It's tough, man. Everything is opposite and messy.'

'Yes, blame the system. We all know what a great driver you are!'

'I was a good driver! I mean I am. *I am* a good driver,' Lavanya insisted. 'I only need to get used to the roads again. You will see.'

'Sure. If you don't need anything, let's get out of here?' Shourya grasped her elbow and guided her towards the exit.

'So what have you been up to?'

'I graduated from UC Berkeley, did an internship at a financial company in Fremont for three months and now I'm working with SQ Inc.'

'Impressive. In Berkeley? How is the Bay Area?' Lavanya asked. 'I have always wanted to travel to the West coast.'

'You should. It's beautiful. But I guess you're used to the bustling New York life by now. I hear you're working at Paxton-Stark-Meester?' Shourya said, and before she could decide how to respond to that, added, 'Funny name, though, isn't it? Abbreviation sounds like PMS.'

'Wow. You always have been classy!'

'I know, right?' he grinned.

They walked out of the store together. As the sunlight hit his face, Lavanya saw his eyes change shades—they looked much lighter than before.

'Did you walk here? Please say you walked here,' she said.

'I walked here.'

'Oh, thank God! Then you can drive the stupid car back to my place. I don't think I'd be able to handle another half hour driving back.'

'Half hour? Your place is five minutes away!'

'Darn it. I didn't need to tell you that.'

'No, you didn't. Hand 'em over.' Shourya's lips stretched in another wide smile as he took the keys from her and walked towards the car. 'It's so good to have you back in my life.'

~

As he drove away from the parking lot, Shourya looked at Lavanya's hands, clasped together in her lap, her knuckles nearly white. She kept picking at her cuticles with her nails, and chipping away her nail polish. Something was up. He wanted to ask her what it was, but they had not spoken at all to each other in so many years, he did not want to inadvertently put her in an uncomfortable position.

'The past four days here alone almost killed me,' he continued instead.

'But you're here for Shreela's wedding! Isn't she around?' Lavanya asked, her eyes shifting to his mane.

Shourya ran a hand through hair self-consciously. 'She's always around. Always. And Mom. They've both made it impossible for a man to survive in the same house as them.'

'Wedding disagreements?'

'Disagreements? They are more like wars! I can't wait for all of this to be over.'

'That bad, huh?' Lavanya stuck out her bottom lip in a half-sympathetic and half-teasing gesture. 'How is everyone? It's been so long since I saw them.'

'Don't worry; you're going to see them a lot from now. I'm officially appointing you my buffer, starting now. Your job is to make my life at home bearable,' Shourya declared.

'Because I do not have anything else to do in *my* life?'

'Do you?' He looked at her challengingly for a second before turning his attention back to the road. 'Please, enlighten me about your grand plans.'

'I do not need to have any grand plans; that's the beauty of being on a vacation, isn't it? I get to have no plans.'

'You always have a plan, Lavanya.'

He had meant that as a light-hearted comment, but she went quiet. There was an awkward silence in the car, which was broken only when Lavanya whispered, 'Maybe this time I don't,' just as he pulled into her driveway.

He nodded, not knowing what she meant. What kind of response was that? It wasn't *what* she said, as much as the *way* she said it that struck him. She was the kind of person who contained a lot of silent drama. She had called *him* dramatic on occasion, but it was she who hid a mountain of theatre inside. Like she would not ask him to shut up and mind his own business. Instead, she would go all silent and brooding on him for a while, and then whisper something softly. *Who does that?*

Shourya had always hated it when she hid something from him. Not because he thought she was obliged to tell him everything, of course not, but because she did not do a great job of hiding anything successfully. So he'd always ended up knowing that something was up, but not what it was. And even when he could ask her what the matter was, he preferred to give her time. If and when she felt comfortable enough to share, she did. It was better that way.

When they got out of the car, Shourya said, 'I don't see my parents' car around; they must have left. I'll walk home from here.'

'What, no! You can't do that!'

'Whoa,' Shourya said. He looked at Lavanya over the hood of the car. Her face was flushed. 'Why . . . what's up?'

'I just . . . I mean, why don't you come in for a while? You cannot go away so soon. We just met!'

'I was going to take your number and call you later. I need to get back home. I have a meeting with the florist; it's urgent.'

'Oh . . . right. There is a wedding in your family. There must be so much work to do . . . What was I thinking . . .?' Lavanya shook her head, her face reddening.

Shourya laughed. 'I was kidding! I would use any available excuse to avoid going back into that battlefield.'

'Then come in for breakfast.'

'I've already had breakfast, but okay. I do miss your mom's cooking.'

Shourya walked up the three steps on the small porch that led to the front door. He had sat on these steps with Lavanya innumerable times as a teenager. He used to walk her home on their way back from school every day, and every day she would insist that he stay for just a few more minutes, always trying to delay going inside for as long as she could. The afternoon sun would be scorching and he would be tired from his cricket practice, but he always stuck around, preparing her to go inside and fight her battle.

Lavanya unlocked the door and pushed it open. 'Come,' she barely whispered.

She never liked going in. Shourya put his hand on her waist and walked inside, coaxing her along.

'Everything looks so different,' he pointed out, pausing after two steps. 'What's with the puke-coloured curtains?'

'Shh! Mom does not take criticism kindly.'

Shourya laughed, looking around. 'But really, so much has changed. Don't you get that feeling when you come back now?'

'Hmm.'

'I mean, it's a lot to take in for me because I'm visiting your place after almost a decade. Well, not really; I was here just an hour ago. But maybe you don't notice that much of a difference. How often do you come home, anyway?'

'Lavi, is that you?' Lavanya's mother called from the first floor, appearing on the stairs a minute later. 'I was about to call you. You haven't eaten anything since the morning. Aren't you hungry? You should . . . Oh, are you with someone?'

'Hello, Aunty,' Shourya said, walking towards her with a wide grin.

'Shourya, you found her then,' Mrs Suryavanshi walked down the stairs.

'Yes, but I came because I need another hug.' He enveloped Mrs Suryavanshi in a bear hug, and she hugged him back with equal enthusiasm.

'Ugh, you should have been *his* mom,' Lavanya rolled her eyes, observing from a distance, her hip resting against the door frame, her arms folded.

'Jealous?' Shourya asked her, resting his chin on top of Mrs Suryavanshi's head, still holding her in a bear hug.

'As if.'

'Oh, you two! Will you ever stop fighting like little kids?' Mrs Suryavanshi shook her head, but she was smiling; she had always enjoyed their constant bickering. She extracted herself from Shourya's arms and studied his face. 'How have you been, beta? You look so thin!'

'Don't mind her, Shourya,' Lavanya interjected. 'Everyone looks thin to her. Anyone whom she does not feed every day is too thin.'

'Actually, I do think I am getting too thin. What do you have for me, Aunty?'

'Ah, such a good child. See, Lavi? Learn something from him. Come in, come in,' she herded the two of them towards the kitchen. 'She does not eat properly. I keep telling her, but she never listens.'

'That's not nice, Lavanya. Not nice at all. You should listen to your mother.'

Lavanya narrowed her eyes at him.

'Sit, sit. Let me heat up breakfast for you. I made aloo parathas and fresh white butter.'

'Yum! See this is what we miss in the States. Starting the day with greasy, buttery food that fills you up till dinnertime.'

'Don't you like aloo parathas?' Mrs Suryavanshi looked offended.

'*I* love them,' Lavanya chipped in, taking advantage of the situation.

'Me too! They are my absolute favourite!' Shourya smirked at Lavanya. 'I was just saying how different food habits are in the States. You know . . . fruit juice, milk, toast, cereal, eggs—nothing too heavy. Ah, those people have nothing on us.'

'Pancakes aren't that light. And bacon,' Lavanya said.

Shourya gasped. 'Bacon! Are you telling me, Lavanya Suryavanshi, that you have taken to eating beef? Beef?! Cow meat?'

Mrs Suryavanshi spun around. Her hand shot to her mouth, eyes wide, as she stared at Lavanya. '*Lavi!*'

'What, *no*! I do not even eat pork, let alone beef. I do not even know what bacon is; only that it is meat. Mom, really!'

Mrs Suryavanshi shook her head. 'Lavi, what is this I'm hearing? Is this how I raised you?'

'Yes, *Lavi*,' Shourya said in an exaggerated tone, 'I never expected you to become so detached from your own culture and values to be okay with eating cow meat. I am *so* disappointed in you.'

'But, I don't even . . . Mom, trust me. Don't listen to him. You know his lifelong agenda is to turn you against me.' Lavanya glared at Shourya. 'I do not eat bacon. I've never had anything other than chicken and fish. I've never even tasted red meat!'

Mrs Suryavanshi did not look convinced. 'I want to believe you . . .'

'You should!'

'Yes, Aunty, you should,' Shourya said, peeling an orange. 'She clearly has no knowledge about red meat.'

'Yes— Wait, what?' Lavanya paused.

'Yup, bacon isn't beef; it's pork. I was just testing you.'

'Wow. And if I'd said bacon is not beef, that would have meant what? That I've eaten it? That's pure genius,' she sneered good-naturedly at Shourya.

'Nah! I know you don't have the balls to try anything that's not approved and permitted. I just wanted to freak you out.'

'You know nothing.'

'Don't I? Do you have secrets now?' Shourya raised one eyebrow.

'Five minutes in, and you kids are already at each other's throats.' Mrs Suryavanshi served hot parathas on the kitchen counter. 'Eat now, before it gets cold.'

'He started it,' Lavanya muttered before sitting down next to Shourya on a tall counter stool. She placed a hot paratha on her plate, plonked a dollop of white butter on top of it and watched it melt away slowly, spreading across the paratha, and eventually seeping out. 'Just how I like it,' she grinned at her mother and picked up her fork and knife.

'What are you doing—?' Shourya interrupted, aghast, before she could take her first bite. 'That is not how you eat a paratha!' He tore a piece of his paratha with his fingers, dipped it in butter and deposited it into his mouth. 'That's how it's done.'

'It's bad manners to talk with your mouth full.' Lavanya continued eating with her fork.

'Use your hands. Trust me, it'll taste better that way!'

'I am eating the exact same thing. The method of eating is not going to affect the taste.'

'Fine. You're only ruining it for yourself.' Shourya knew she was not going to do it his way now, especially because he had asked her to.

'I am not.' Lavanya turned to her mother and said, 'It is delicious, Mom. Have you eaten?'

'Yes, I ate with your father. He got late for work after all. His car would not start again; it has been giving him so much trouble recently.'

'Why, what's wrong?' Lavanya asked between bites.

'It is so old. I keep telling him to buy a new one, but he never listens. He takes my car when I am not using it.'

'Why didn't you tell me when I was taking your car in the morning? I could have walked,' Lavanya did not look up from her plate.

'Oh, he did not want to bother you . . .'

Shourya noticed Lavanya's lower lip twitch. Her hands stalled next to her plate for a moment, and then it passed. She nodded and resumed eating.

'Aunty, this really is delicious,' Shourya said brightly.

'Take one more, beta,' Mrs Suryavanshi said, and put another paratha on his plate.

Shourya did not understand what had happened, but the air in the room felt thick with stress. They had shifted from a comfortable, warm atmosphere to a chilly one in a matter of seconds. He tried to get everyone to talk again, but his cheer felt forced.

After breakfast, Shourya got up to leave and Lavanya walked him to the door. He paused at the front steps, the very spot where they had shared so many secrets and worries. It may have been a different time, but he wondered if the ghosts haunting Lavanya were still the same.

As if sensing what he was about to ask, Lavanya murmured, 'Not now, Shourya.'

He tried to read her expression, but she was making it impossible—looking away from him, her face blank.

'Are you still—?' he began to ask, but she cut him off.

'Give me your phone.'

When he handed it over, she saved her number into his contacts list and placed it back in his palm, holding his hand for a second before pulling away.

'Call me soon?' Lavanya asked, looking up at him, a half-smile on her face. Then, without waiting for his response, she turned around and went back inside.

5

'It's really not my thing,' she insisted.

'It's every lawyer's thing,' the handsome man with the tiny ponytail persisted.

'Thank you, but not me.'

'Your call,' he shrugged. 'But keep this. Let me know if you change your mind.'

'I won't . . .'

But he was already gone. She got off the bar stool, wobbling for a moment on her five-inch heels. She looked over at the table in the corner where her colleagues from PSM were sitting. This was the hub for lawyers, most of them turning to alcohol and cocaine after the end of every week. She was never welcome there.

As she stepped out of the pub, the wind blew her hair away from her face. The napkin with the hastily scrawled phone number was still in her hand. She pocketed it.

Lavanya was having trouble opening her eyes. Her forehead felt all scrunched up, as if it had been like that for hours. She tried to relax her forehead muscles, but failed. She tried to smoothen them out with her fingers but they went back to being a furrow within a matter of seconds.

She fumbled with the comforter, trying to reach her cell phone. The satin of the bed sheet felt cool to her warm fingers before they landed on the hard metallic phone. The digits popping up in front of her New York skyline wallpaper told her it was 1.23 p.m.

She groaned.

Her throat was dry; she had been breathing through her mouth all night, and her nose was blocked. Having lived in New York for the past year, she had arrogantly assumed a fleece sweatshirt would be enough protection against the Delhi cold.

She sat up and lowered her feet to the floor. The tiles were freezing and she quickly pulled her legs up and tucked them under her to warm them. She sat there, trying to make sense of time and place, breathing heavily, too warm under the comforter. When she felt like she could get up without keeling over, she tentatively pulled one foot from under her butt and then another. She managed to stand up, and walk to the window. There was a water bottle on the windowsill. After gulping down some water, she felt her nostrils opening up for air again.

She put on her slippers and walked to the bathroom. She never looked in the mirror any more. Since finding out about her disease, every time she saw her reflection, she imagined some sign or other on her face that would indicate how her condition was getting worse. She would invent lines and spots and blemishes, and would convince herself her health was deteriorating every second. Before long, she would go into full-blown panic mode, and that was never good, especially when she was trying desperately to conquer a fatal condition by refusing to think about it.

She took her time, cleaning her teeth, then her body and her hair, attempting to wash off her disease. At the very least she had hoped it would make her feel cleaner, lighter, but at the end of the hot shower all she felt was a cold shiver and a runny nose. She wrapped herself in her old bathrobe, the one with Dora the Explorer on it that she had had since she was ten; it barely fit her now. She had never seen the cartoon, but begged her mother to buy it; she had been enchanted with Dora's huge eyes.

'I thought I heard you move around,' her mother was at the door, peeking into her bedroom.

'Morning, Mom,' Lavanya mumbled, her throat feeling rough and torn.

'Is everything okay? Why are your eyes so swollen? Have you been crying?' Mrs Suryavanshi held her daughter by her shoulders and peered into her eyes.

'No, my migraine's giving me trouble. And I think I caught a cold. That's all.' Lavanya forced her eyes to open wide in an attempt to flatten her forehead again.

'I told you to wear a hat. You never listen. I thought something was wrong when you did not wake up in the morning, but you were up till late last night, weren't you? I saw light coming from under your door.'

'Mom, you worry too much. I'm okay. You don't have to stay up to see what time I go to sleep,' Lavanya chuckled.

'Beta . . .' Mrs Suryavanshi had a grim expression on her face. She held Lavanya's arm and prodded her towards the bed. 'Come, sit with me.'

Lavanya tried to compose her expression. She knew what her mother wanted to talk about; she could see her forehead scrunched up the same way her own had been when she woke up. She took a slow breath, struggling to remain calm . . . at least on the outside. She sat down next to her mother on the bed, her hands clasped together on her lap, as if drawing support from one another.

'Lavi, you know that your father and I are very happy that you have come home, don't you?'

Lavanya felt her cheeks burn. Her mother was looking at her, but Lavanya could not meet her eyes. She was staring pointedly at her hands, the fingers entwined, holding on for dear life. She nodded.

'When you left . . . the house felt empty. It *was* empty. The silence was sheer torture. We took a lot of time to adjust to it. I thought I had got used to it . . . but now . . . now that you are here . . .' Mrs Suryavanshi looked away.

Once she stopped feeling her mother's gaze piercing her skin, Lavanya felt confident enough to look at her.

'What I am trying to ask you is . . . is everything okay with you? I do not know what to think any more. I have not seen you in so long, I cannot tell if this is how you are now, or if something is bothering you. Whatever it is, you can always tell me . . .'

This time when her mother's eyes examined her, Lavanya did not turn away. She knew if she did now, she would give herself away. She had always been a terrible liar and her mother, especially, could see right through her.

'Relax, Mom. Nothing is wrong. I know you're probably wondering why I am here . . . I am asking myself that too, trust me. I ask myself that every day. I guess I just missed everyone so much. It had been too long . . .' Lavanya said.

'Yes, it had.' Her mother nodded solemnly.

'But I am here now. Please don't be sad. I know I should have come sooner . . . but I did not know how to, I mean, it was not easy for me to do. And I was trying to concentrate on my studies. Harvard Law is no joke. I came so close to giving up so many times.'

'Oh, you are a brilliant student. I am sure it wasn't anything you couldn't handle.'

Lavanya's throat choked at the pride in her mother's voice. 'It was too much sometimes, Mom. I had to give it everything I had to get through.'

'I can understand that. I am not blaming you. I only wished that you would call more often. I have missed you.'

Her mother looked old. Under the bright light coming from the window, Lavanya noticed for the first time the brown spots on the mounds of her mother's cheeks, and how the creases around her eyes and lips had become much more pronounced. Her skin was not as tight and glowing as Lavanya remembered. She felt guilty for leaving her mother to grow old alone.

'I missed you too, Mom.' She barely managed to say the words. She could see her mother's eyes shine with unshed tears. Lavanya ached knowing what she had inadvertently done to her mother by going so far away, for far too long. But she had not had a choice. She just had to get away from this place, and everything that had happened since, however painful, was collateral damage.

Mrs Suryavanshi blinked away the tears from her eyes, and asked, 'What are your plans, Lavi? How long are you here for? We want you to stay with us for as long as you can, but of course, you have a job and a life to get back to. I would like to be prepared for your departure this time.'

'I, uh . . . I am here till the end of the month. Till New Year's. Or maybe till the first week of January? I'm not sure about my plans yet.'

'Have you taken leave from work?'

Lavanya recalled the nasty exchange she had had with Mr Cather the last time she was at the Paxton-Stark-Meester offices. 'Sort of.'

'Okay. I hope your boss lets you extend your leave.'

'Me too.'

Mrs Suryavanshi opened her mouth to speak, then shut it again, as if deciding against whatever she was planning to say.

'Please don't worry so much,' offered Lavanya, 'I am perfectly fine.'

Her mother did not look convinced. 'Why do I feel like you are hiding something?'

'You always feel that way, but I am not. It has been so long since I was here last. That is why I am a little . . . confused, I guess? You know, this is all a little overwhelming,' Lavanya gestured to the room in general. There was an old tattoo on her bedpost, barely visible. It looked like some sort of fantastical dragon-like creature. She remembered getting the temporary tattoo free with a stick of gum as a child. She ran her finger over what was left of the tattoo. 'So many memories.'

Mrs Suryavanshi smiled. 'You used to put these ghastly tattoos everywhere around the house. And they are so tough to clean! Remember the heated conversations we would have about that?'

'Why do you want to take them out? They are ugly, but they are cool.'

'That reminds me, do you want to go through some of your stuff?'

'What kind of stuff?'

'We gave away most of your old clothes and shoes, but the rest is all here—your toys, photo albums, books, diaries, CDs, junk jewellery . . . all your things. I think you'll feel better looking through them.' Mrs Suryavanshi pulled out the under-bed storage, adding softly, 'I know I do.'

Lavanya could see her worn-out pink journal and her *Titanic* DVD in the box her mother opened up. She smiled tentatively. 'Why not?'

~

Shourya was having a good day. His mother and sister had agreed on everything so far, minus a few minor conflicts that were resolved without any major hiccups. He had taken

Shreela and her fiancé Manav out for dinner, and was happy and relieved to find that they seemed to enjoy each other's company. Shreela could be very stubborn and unreasonable at times, but Manav seemed like the kind of person who could handle that. Shourya had had reservations about the man his sister was marrying, reservations that had nothing to do with Manav per se. He was sure he would have had the same reservations about any man Shreela chose. But he could see that they adored each other, and his little sister looked ecstatic in Manav's presence. He sighed with satisfaction. The evening had gone better than he could have hoped for. If anything, it had ended too soon. He checked the time as he parked the car.

'It's not even ten!' he exclaimed.

'I'm so sorry Manav had to go back early. This almost never happens. It's just that the project he's working on is about to end, so it's getting a bit intense,' Shreela said, as she attempted to unbuckle her seatbelt.

'I know. You don't have to defend him.'

'I'm just saying.'

'I only meant that we could go out and do something. This is a waste of a perfectly good night. What are your plans?'

'To. Get. Out. Of. This. Damn—' Shreela jerked the seatbelt repeatedly in frustration. 'Argh! Stupid thing.'

'You don't even know how to get out of a *stupid* seatbelt, how are you supposed to be someone's wife?' Shourya unsnapped her belt.

'So? That makes things all the more easy. Manav will be there to help me with my seatbelt and stuff. Besides, we will get a better car, one with seatbelts that work.'

'Hey, what's wrong with this car?' Shourya asked indignantly, stepping out and observing the red SUV. 'Mom and Dad love it.'

'No, they don't. They only tell you they do because you gifted it to them. What else can they say?'

'What! I never knew they did not like it. Why didn't you tell me? I could've got this replaced.'

'It doesn't matter to them what car they are in, as long as it takes them where they want to go. Now, let's go inside. I'm freezing.' Shreela tugged at the sleeve of his shirt.

'Of course you are. It's the middle of December and you're wearing just a silk wrap over your dress. What did you think was going to happen?'

'It's a scarf. And it's Hermes. And it was a gift from Manav. I can tolerate a little cold to show it off!'

'Makes so much sense.' Shourya rolled his eyes. He put his arm around her and steered her into the elevator.

'Oh, did you hear from the photographer? I can't have the wedding if Karan Dhillon isn't the one filming it. I just *can't*.'

Shourya had forgotten about the photographer. 'He hasn't called me back.'

'Liar! You were supposed to look up his email address on his Facebook fan page and write to him. You never contacted him, did you?'

'I did!'

'You didn't!'

'Fine, I didn't. But I'll do it right now.' Shourya pulled out his cell phone and launched Facebook. 'What's his name again?'

'Karan Dhillon.' Shreela dug for the keys in her giant bag and unlocked the door. 'He must have a million likes on his Facebook page. He's amazing! He has filmed so many celebrity weddings. Thankfully, he is my friend's friend's cousin, and she has already spoken to him about doing my wedding, otherwise it's impossible to get him at such short noti— Bhaiya? What's wrong?'

'Huh?' Shourya glanced up from his phone. 'Noth . . . nothing . . .' he said distractedly. He turned back to the image open on his screen.

Deepti and Avik.

Engaged.

'Are you sure? You look like . . . I don't know. You look weird.' Shreela peered at him uncertainly.

'Yeah. Yeah, I'm okay.' Shourya said in a clipped tone. 'Listen, why don't you go on in, and I'll . . . be back . . . soon?'

'What happened, Bhaiya, are you okay?'

'Of course. I forgot something. Be back soon.' Shourya hurried out of the corridor and into the elevator. He felt stifled. He needed air.

Engaged.

He dashed across the parking lot towards the car. He needed to run, but his legs suddenly felt heavy, restricting his motion. He slammed the door and floored the accelerator, speeding away into the dark.

Shourya drove around the city for over an hour, aimlessly looping around in circles, cursing the vehicles stalled at traffic signals, honking incessantly. He knew he should not be so bothered, that the news should not affect him, but at the very least he had thought Deepti would have the decency to tell him about it rather than let him find out from Facebook. Pictures of the happy couple on a holiday cruise showing off bright smiles and an even brighter diamond—not what he had expected to see when he logged on.

When he had exhausted his adrenaline burst, he found himself slowing down in front of a familiar house. He kept sitting in the car, breathing hard, trying to get his chaotic emotions under control. This was the end. Things had been over between Deepti and him a long time ago, but it was official now. Their lives were going in different directions, and there was no way they could go back to being what they were once no matter how good it was or how much he wished they would. They were independent of each other now, free.

Then why did he not feel free? Why did he feel so trapped?

He honked one more time before getting out of the car. The front gate was locked. 'No. No, no, no,' he muttered, before yelling, 'LAVANYA!' He was lost. He did not know where to go from there. He knew he could not go back home; Shreela would grill him for hours till he told her what was wrong and then she would treat him differently. He did not want to take away from her pre-wedding bliss. And if he got back on the road again, he would probably kill someone or get himself killed. 'Lavanya!' he shouted again.

He shook the metal gate, making it rattle.

'Lavanya!'

The small porch light came on and front door opened. He saw Mrs Suryavanshi search the source of the commotion in the darkness. 'Who is there?'

'Aunty, is Lavanya home?'

'Shourya? Is everything okay?'

'Yes. Is Lavanya home?' he asked again.

'Lavi!' Mrs Suryavanshi called, turning towards the upper floor balcony. 'I'll go get her.'

A minute later, Lavanya appeared at the door, wearing a black sweatshirt and grey sweatpants. She padded towards the gate on bare feet and unlocked it.

'Shourya? What's going on?' she asked. She looked up at him and examined his face. 'Are you all right?'

He pulled the gate open and took a step towards her. The words were caught in his throat. He was not the type of person who cried, but the concern in Lavanya's voice brought him dangerously close to tears. He pursed his lips and shook his head.

'Hey, Sho—'

Before she could finish, he had pulled her into a hug. They stood like that for a long time—Shourya resting his head over her shoulder, his eyes closed, leaning on her, his breath coming in short, crisp gasps. Eventually, he could feel some of the tension exiting his body. He felt Lavanya's arms tighten around him before she let go.

'Shourya?' her voice was muffled.

'Hmm?'

'As much as I love standing here out in the cold and dark with you, I can't feel my toes any more.'

Shourya snorted and released her.

'Seriously. You need to learn how to hug someone a head shorter than you; you'll choke someone to death some day. Can we go inside now? I am freezing here.'

'You, melodramatic creature, you,' Shourya returned, his lips curving slightly.

'I did make you smile though.' She looked very pleased with herself.

Shourya let her drag him inside with her.

6

Lavanya shut the door to her bedroom and turned to Shourya. She had seen him this agitated before, and it had always been momentary. He used to get in and out of that zone very swiftly. But she could sense something deeper that night. His ears were red and she had felt his body tremble when he had hugged her.

'Could it be any darker in here? What are you doing, saving electricity or something?' Shourya commented, glancing around the room. He picked up a book from her desk and flipped the pages before placing it back and turning his attention to her oversized headphones.

He was looking everywhere other than at her. But Lavanya was not about to let it go. She sat down at the foot of the bed and watched him. He was now studying her iPad. 'What can your passcode be?'

'Shourya.'

'Hmm?'

'Look at me.'

He glanced at her, without making eye contact and then focused on her iPad again. He kept the gadget back and looked at the ceiling, exhaling loudly.

'Come here,' Lavanya coaxed. 'Talk to me.'

Shourya walked towards the window and plonked down on the windowsill. When he pulled open the drapes, pieces of paper flew from behind it and landed on the floor. 'Oh, sorry.' He bent to pick them up, but Lavanya rushed and gathered them up before him.

'What is that?' he asked.

'Nothing.'

'Then why are you hiding it? Show me.'

'Fine. First you tell me what is going on with you,' she said, trying to keep calm. She reclaimed her position at the foot of the bed, discreetly slipping one of the sheets of paper under the covers, while folding the rest and keeping them on her lap.

Shourya eyed the papers she was holding. He seemed to think for a minute, before saying, 'Fine. I was going to tell you anyway.'

He sat next to her on the bed and sighed, as if to prepare himself.

'Go on,' she prodded.

'Can you not look at me like that?'

'Like what? With my eyes? That is how I see things.'

'Haha,' he said dryly. 'Seriously. You can't look at me or interrupt me. I've never talked about this . . . stuff before. Stop looking at me like that.'

'How can you tell I am looking at you? You are staring at that vase!' Lavanya could feel her frustration mounting with all the secrecy and weirdness.

'I can feel your eyes burn into me.'

'Oh, shut up!'

'Just stop looking at me, okay? You stare at the vase too.'

Lavanya looked away from him, giving up. This was not how people talked, looking away from each other. But something was upsetting him and she wanted to help, so she

did as he asked. 'Staring at the vase. Feel free to start whenever
. . .' she said, and saw him nod out of the corner of her eyes.

He spoke up after a minute. 'When you left, it was as if
you'd not just left the country, but the planet. I know you
wanted to get out of here desperately and I know you had a lot
on your hands, trying to adjust to living in a foreign country
by yourself and your studies, but . . . anyway. I saw her in my
first semester. This girl, she was amazing. You remember Kara,
the girl I dated briefly back in high school? I used to think I
was in love with her, but when I saw Deepti I realized what I
felt for Kara wasn't really love. Not even close. Do you know
what I'm saying?' He suddenly turned to Lavanya.

'Not entirely, but mostly.' She continued staring at the
vase. 'I am not allowed to speak and ask questions though,
am I?'

'What I mean is, I thought breaking up with Kara was
tough, but when I met Deepti, it was as if everything changed.
We were put in the same project in our second semester and
I could not stand being around her but not *with* her. It was
torture. She was in a long-term relationship with this guy, her
high school sweetheart. I tried to stay away from her when I
found out about them. But I couldn't. And then, when we
became friends, I could see how unhappy she was with him. I
couldn't bear to see her so sad all the time.'

'Ugh. Tell me you did *not*.'

'You're not supposed to speak!' Shourya snapped.

'You did not break them up, did you? That is not a nice
thing to do.'

'I didn't *do* anything. Not anything she didn't want,
anyway. We were getting closer to each other every day, and
I could tell she had developed feelings for me too. So one day,
I told her how I felt.'

'Not cool.'

'What was I supposed to do?' Shourya demanded. 'Hide my feelings forever? And see her hurt and sad because of her asshole boyfriend every single day? He was possessive, overbearing, insecure. He was paranoid and he let out all his bullshit on her *every* day. Her eyes were swollen from crying all the time, she stopped coming to college regularly. Her performance in tests was going down. When she was not there, I realized she deserved so much better than him; I knew she should be with me. I would never hurt her the way he did!' he finished, his tone urgent towards the end.

Lavanya chose to stay silent.

'Anyway. Their relationship came to its inevitable end. It took me about six months after that to convince her to go out with me. I couldn't have been happier, Lavanya. It was so great.' Shourya sighed.

Lavanya felt a pang of envy. They had spent all their time together for years, but she had missed out on so much after she left Delhi. They were in school when Shourya began dating Kara, and it was nowhere as intense as this thing with Deepti sounded. She had liked Kara, but never thought she was worthy of him. They were too uninvolved in each other's lives. It was as if they were playing each other's boyfriend and girlfriend simply because everyone in school was doing it, without any real feelings for the other.

'We were together throughout college. Towards the end, I started preparing for my GRE. You know how you always talked about Harvard Law School? Somehow, I think it seeped into my mind and became my dream too. Not law, of course. I wanted to join a master's programme in business finance from there. I think the thought first occurred to me after you left. I wanted to come there too. Four years after you, but still,' Shourya chuckled.

Lavanya found herself smiling. She had hated herself for deserting him the way she had.

'Towards the end of college, I convinced Deepti to come with me too. I tutored her, and we took our tests together. I know she did not care as much about Harvard as I did, or even studying abroad for that matter. Her score wasn't good enough for Harvard, but she did get into a bunch of other great universities. UC Berkeley was the only university we both cracked. So—'

'*No!*' Lavanya burst out.

'What?'

'Tell me you did not give up Harvard for a *girl!*' She spat out the last word as if it were poison.

'I loved her, Lavanya. You can't imagine how it was. I would have done anything for her. I really, really loved her.'

'Enough to pass up on your dream university, evidently,' she said, gritting her teeth. 'Yet you say *loved*. Past tense . . .'

'I did everything I could. I gave her everything she wanted, everything I had.' Shourya's voice was low. Lavanya could not help turning to look at him.

He exhaled loudly and fell back on the bed, avoiding her eyes, his own trained on the ceiling. She looked at him. His tall frame was unfolded on her bed and his feet touched the floor. She could see his chest rise and fall as he breathed. He was dressed sharply, in a blue shirt and black trousers. But the first two buttons of his shirt were undone and the sleeves rolled up to his elbows. His dinner jacket was now lying on the only chair in her room. He was probably on his way to or coming from somewhere, but something had messed his night up.

She lay down next to him and asked, 'What happened?' She continued looking at him, and he kept his eyes closed.

'She says she fell in love with my roommate in grad school . . .' Shourya gulped.

Lavanya put her hand on his, and squeezed. He did not respond. As he told her the details, it seemed as if he was in some other world, one he did not like visiting. She continued to hold his hand nonetheless.

'I saw them together shortly after. She cried, she begged and pleaded. She wanted me to forgive her and take her back. I tried . . . but I couldn't do it,' Shourya balled up his hands in a fist, locking Lavanya's hand inside. 'Meanwhile, Avik obviously found out the entire story and was more forgiving towards Deepti. Their *relationship* was new and exciting, and she had not betrayed his trust as much as she had mine. Later, she went back to Avik while I was away for my internship.'

'How long ago was this?'

'Eight months,' Shourya said, and then rushed to add, 'I know. I know that's a lot, and I should have been over this by now, but . . . they got engaged, Lavanya. I found out tonight.'

'Did you not know they were still together?'

'I did. Trust me. I live in the same apartment with them, so I do know.'

'What!'

'Yup. Could not afford to move out at the time. I was still a student. So I had to see their love blossom in front of my eyes,' Shourya opened them now and looked at Lavanya. 'But I was not prepared for this—them getting engaged.'

Lavanya's heart sank. What had happened to him was cruel. Yet she did not know what to say. She sat up on the bed, her lips pursed in anger. 'She sounds like a delight, *really, but she's a bitch.*'

'Lavanya!' Shourya sat up too.

'What do you want me to say?!' Lavanya was livid. 'She has been a total jerk, playing you around from the beginning. First, leaving her boyfriend—any girl who dumps her boyfriend for you is likely to dump you for another guy too. Second, stringing you along for six months before agreeing to go on a date with you. Third, not making you go to Harvard. Fourth, lying to all your friends about your relationship. Fifth, cheating on you with your roommate. Sixth, asking you to take her back but then eventually going back to boyfriend number three. And all this is from what I've heard about her in just the last half hour. I'm sure the list gets longer on longer acquaintance.'

'You are judging her. She made some mistakes, but she is a good person.'

'Shourya Kapoor, are you defending your bitch ex-girlfriend right now?' Lavanya could not believe this was happening. *How could someone do so many bad things to you, but you still stand up for them, defend their every action?*

'It's not like that. What if she really did fall in love with Avik? What could she have done——?'

'She could have talked to you!' Lavanya said in exasperation. 'Certainly not cheat on you. Or lie to that other fellow. Not been so ungrateful about the things you did for her. And you, do you see what you are doing here? After all that she's done to you, you still can't hear a word against her. It's like she has this power over you——'

Shourya interrupted Lavanya by raising his hand, 'Okay, fine. Fine! I get it. She's a horrible person. She did a terrible thing to me. But how do I get past that? This is insane. It has been eight months, and I am exactly where she left me. God, this is so humiliating, admitting out loud to someone that I am having trouble moving on from my ex.'

'Shut up. This is me, Shourya,' Lavanya folded her legs and sat facing him. 'You can tell me anything. And this is clearly something big for it to have affected you the way it has. You cannot ignore it and go on living life as if it never happened, like nothing's wrong.' Lavanya paused, realizing the hypocrisy in what she was saying.

'Men are not supposed to be so affected by stuff like this,' Shourya mumbled.

'That's true only for men who are douchebags and don't care about things that matter. You are not one of them. She is someone you've loved for years. You probably had your entire life planned in your head. When something like this happens . . . it ought to change you. And I think . . .' Lavanya sighed. 'See, I am no expert on this relationship stuff; I've never been in one. But I really do think that the only way you are going to get past this and move on is if you acknowledge that it happened, and that it changed you. You can never go back to being who you were before this, but you can be better.'

'Wow. You have become quite the philosopher,' Shourya said, offering a tentative smile.

'Shut up! This is serious.'

Shourya fell silent. He watched the changing expressions on Lavanya's face. He knew she was right. He had never shared all this with anyone. Nor had he expected to feel better after doing it. Surprisingly, talking about it had taken his mind off Deepti and Avik's engagement. He was only thinking about how his story must look like to a third person.

It gave him some much-needed perspective. Maybe there *was* a way out of this mess, after all.

'I am glad I told you,' he said softly. When I saw those engagement pictures tonight, I don't know . . . I could not think of where else to go . . .'

'I am glad you told me too. And that you came here.' Lavanya squeezed his hand, the hand she had been holding all this while.

'Will you help me? I need to get out of this . . . this *thing*, man. It's killing me.'

'I will do whatever I can to help. But like I said, I do not know much about this stuff.'

'You clearly know more about this stuff than me. I could use some help.'

'I do have an idea.'

'I'm already scared.'

Lavanya laughed. 'I make all your relationship decisions from now.'

'That's too much power.'

'That is what the deal is. Take it or leave it.'

'Ferocious, aren't you? I can totally picture you as the PMS corporate lawyer right now,' Shourya winked.

Lavanya ignored his mutilation of PSM. 'Do we have a deal?'

'We do. Now, shake on it.'

'You have to let go of my hand for that. Honestly, Kapoor, the blood flow to my right hand has been cut off for an hour now.'

Shourya released her hand and they shook hands to seal their deal. 'Now it's your turn. Show me what you've got hidden there. I may get distracted, but I never forget.'

Lavanya got up, clutching the papers in her hand, and walked away from the bed.

'You cheater! I told you, now it's your turn. You know I'm not going to let you get away with this,' Shourya got up and lunged for the papers.

Lavanya pulled them away, but said, 'Fine, fine. Only because fair is fair. Here.'

Shourya read out what was on it. 'Learn to play the guitar. Meet Salman Khan. Get a piercing . . . What is this? Some sort of a to-do list?'

'Yup.' Lavanya's face turned red.

Shourya laughed. 'Go on a date with Vishal Madhogharia? Seriously? That cricket captain from high school? I didn't know you had the hots for him.'

'Give it back to me.' Lavanya tried to snatch it back, but he raised his arms up, making it impossible for her to reach the paper. 'You cannot judge me based on this. These lists are from years ago. I used to randomly scribble down stuff I wanted to do some day. I was sixteen . . . maybe seventeen then.'

'Then what are you doing with this now?'

'Well . . . I was looking through some of my old stuff with Mom in the morning and we found this. And I realized I have not done even one of these things. Okay, one—*Visit New York*. But that's it. My entire life, I have not achieved anything. And now, there is no time.'

Shourya laughed. 'Get a leash on all the drama, man. You're talking as if you're dying or something. You still have a lot of time. Relax.'

He noticed Lavanya freeze for a second, and then stammer, 'But, but . . . I wanted to do these things before I turned twenty-five. This is a before-twenty-five list. And I have done none of the things on it.'

'Okay,' Shourya said, observing Lavanya closely. She was definitely hiding something. 'Let's do this then.'

'What?'

'Yes, why not? I am here for two more weeks. What about you?'

Lavanya seemed to think about it for a minute before saying, 'Two or three weeks, I guess. At least till New Year's Eve.'

'Perfect. We'll start working through your list tomorrow,' Shourya said, tossing the list back to her. 'You should put this down on a new sheet of paper, by the way, this one's coming apart.'

'I will. But are you serious?'

'Absolutely. We start tomorrow. Think of this as my end of the deal. You help me move on, I help you complete the tasks on your list. Win-win.'

Lavanya looked unconvinced.

'I'm going home now,' Shourya said. 'I have several missed calls from my distressed sister, but we begin tomorrow. See you.'

And with that, he wished her goodnight and left, feeling much lighter going out of the house than he had coming in.

7

Lavanya slept well that night. When she woke up the morning after, she felt better than she had in a while, her head was not aching and she could breathe through her nose. She took that as a good sign, and in the same spirit, dialled Shourya's number.

''Lo?' came the groggy response.

'Hello! Get up! We had a deal, we have to start today!'

'What are you so chirpy about?' Shourya groaned.

'We are starting today. We had a deal.'

'Stop saying we had a deal.'

'We had a deal,' Lavanya repeated.

'Suryavanshi.'

'Kapoor.'

'If you don't hang up right now and let me sleep, we won't have a deal for much longer,' Shourya threatened.

Lavanya did not say anything.

A few seconds later, Shourya said, 'You've not hung up, have you?'

'No.'

She heard him exhale loudly, followed by the sound of rustling. 'All right then, I'm up. What is the first thing on your list?'

Lavanya pulled out the sheet she had hidden under her bedcover the night before—her 'Lame Girl Dying Wish List' of all the things she wished to do before dying. Compiled from the three short lists she had found from her teenage years. Of course, she had left the 'dying' part out.

'Learn to play the guitar,' Lavanya read out.

'You know you can't excel at playing the guitar overnight, right?'

'I know. But I can start. Besides it won't be that much trouble. You know how to play; you can teach me. Remember back in school I always wanted to learn from you but we never found time? Well, we have time now.'

'Do you want to come over?'

'No, you come here in the evening.'

'Then why the hell did you wake me up now?' he protested indignantly.

Lavanya laughed. 'Go back to sleep. I will see you in the evening.'

She folded the top part of her list, tore away the title, shredded it into tiny pieces and threw them into the trash. She could not have anyone seeing that.

She got out of bed excitedly; she had plans for the day. Shourya had promised to help her complete her list, but she wanted to get a head start on it and she didn't need him for what she had in mind. And it would be a great surprise for him too.

She showered, dressed and ran downstairs, feeling more alive than she had since she got *the news*. It was the first time she did not feel sick, or like she was progressing swiftly towards an impending death.

There was silence in the house. 'Mom?' she called. She had expected her dad to not be there; it was past the time he left for work. But she was surprised to find her mother missing too. 'Mom?'

She went into the kitchen. A plate with halved boiled eggs, almonds and sprouts sat on the table, covered with another plate, and a note beside it. She helped herself to half an egg and read the note. *Gone to school, Mom.* Lavanya remembered her mother telling her she had to go to school early for some event, some kind of a Christmas celebration before the school closed for the winter break.

Lavanya gulped down her breakfast with a glass of orange juice, and called for a cab. The website said her cab would arrive in half an hour. She could not control her excitement. She had wanted a dog ever since she was a child. Back then, her mother had been against the idea because she was working full-time as a school teacher and her father was never home. She reasoned she did not have the time or energy to take care of a pet, and Lavanya was not old enough to be responsible for the dog herself. So she had let it go.

But ever since she had seen the flyer that came with the newspaper, about a six-week-old, three-legged, black bulldog, she had not been able to get his image out of her head. He had a fourth leg, but it was mostly useless. Lavanya wanted to give the poor creature a home. Her mother was only working part-time now, and could use some company. It was too quiet in the house. It was only after her mother had mentioned how hard it had been to get used to living without her that Lavanya realized how she had left the house empty and her mother without a companion when she left for the US. Ever since then, every moment of silence in the house was doubly pronounced for her.

Getting a dog would be the perfect solution for that. She did not know how long she had, and she could not leave her mother alone again. When she saw the flyer with the little puppy's picture on it, her decision was made. She could not think of a better plan.

When her cab arrived, she jumped off her chair and dashed out. She gave the cab driver the address and waited anxiously to meet the new addition to their family and bring the little guy home.

~

'Lavi?' Mrs Suryavanshi called. 'Are you home?'

Lavanya whispered, 'Down, boy,' to the tiny ball of energy that was jumping around her excitedly. 'Yeah, upstairs. I'll be down in a minute. There's someone I would like you to meet.'

'Who is it?'

'Just a second. I'm bringing him down.' Lavanya could barely conceal the excitement in her voice.

She cradled the puppy in her arms and walked down the stairs carefully. He snuggled his head into her arm. They had spent just five hours together, but it felt like they had known each other forever.

'Who—?' Her mother paused. '*What is that?*'

'Mom, meet Toughy,' Lavanya grinned at the shocked and horrified expression on her mother's face. She lifted her arms and brought the puppy forward. 'Toughy, this is your new mom.'

'What do you mean by that? Is it going to live here with us?'

'Toughy's a *he*. Don't be mean!'

'Lavi, I have told you I do not want a dog. I cannot look after him. It is too much work. Plus you know I am scared of dogs!' Mrs Suryavanshi had panic written all over her face.

'No, you've never told me that! You always said you don't have time to look after a pet. But now you do. Besides, it's high time you hired a full-time maid to take care of things around here. You should not have to do everything on your own,' Lavanya suggested.

'I do have a full-time maid, Sangeeta. Her sister just had a baby, so she is on a leave, taking care of her. But she'll be back in a week.'

'There you go. Problem solved.'

'But I cannot be around dogs. They have very sharp teeth.'

Lavanya chuckled. 'You're being such a child, Mom. Toughy is never going to hurt you. The poor puppy just needs love.' Lavanya bent and put him down on the floor.

'Where did you get it . . . uh, *him* from?' Mrs Suryavanshi took a step back and Toughy limped towards her.

'Mom, let him smell you. He is just trying to get familiar. I found a flyer with the newspaper. He is only six weeks old. If someone didn't adopt him, the owner was going to have him put down.'

Toughy sniffed Mrs Suryavanshi and then hobbled around her in circles, the same way he'd been doing with Lavanya upstairs.

'See, he likes you!' Lavanya bent down and scratched his neck. 'Do this, he likes that.'

'No!' her mother looked terrified.

'He won't bite you. He's just a puppy. Once you get to know him, you will fall in love.' Lavanya pulled Toughy up and held his good front foot out. 'And this tough guy is just the best.'

Her mother still did not look convinced.

'Come on, Mom. Just touch his belly once, you will see.'

Mrs Suryavanshi crouched down next to Lavanya hesitantly. She reached for Toughy's stomach, touching him first with one finger and then her entire palm. She rubbed his tummy, a slow smile spreading through her face as he lolled his head back and wagged his tail in delight.

Lavanya met her eye, grinning widely. 'How do you like your gift?'

Her mother smiled back.

~

Shourya dropped Shreela off at the tailor's for the final fitting of her wedding lehenga. Hopefully, this chapter in the wedding planner would be closed by the end of the day. Choosing the lehenga had taken Shreela three months. She had searched every store in Chandni Chowk before flying to Mumbai and checking every store there, followed by a trip to Kolkata. She had gone around in circles three times before final selecting one from Delhi. When Shourya heard this, he counted his blessings for not having been here to witness it.

'Take care, Bhaiya,' Shreela said as she hopped out of the car.

'Yeah, yeah,' he rolled his eyes.

When he had returned home the previous night, she was still up, as he had suspected. However, surprisingly, she did not grill him too much about what it was that upset him. She only wanted to know if he was feeling better and when he told her he was, she seemed to buy it. He had told her he had met Lavanya, and that seemed to convince her that all was well.

'Do you want me to come inside with you?' he asked half-heartedly.

'No, it's okay. My friends will be here in a minute.'

'Thank you,' Shourya grinned, relieved he did not have to sit through any part of a fitting session.

Shreela made a face at him and waved goodbye as he pulled away from the store and headed towards Lavanya's house. Shreela's wedding was only five days away, and he had been caught up all day, getting all the preparations in place.

Organizing a wedding was no mean feat. He had insisted on hiring an agency, but both his mother and sister wanted to do it themselves, saying it was too important an event to let someone else handle it. Of course, 'themselves' really meant Shourya, and all of it ended up falling on his shoulders. He was happy with the way things were going. Unless there was a last-minute emergency, everything seemed on track for the wedding. He was amazed at himself for pulling things off with time to spare.

It had been nice to hear Lavanya sound so happy that morning, for a change. She had been texting him all day, asking him to come soon, saying she wanted to show him something. He wondered what it could be.

He found out soon enough. As he pulled up in front of her house, he saw a small bulldog hobbling up and down the front yard. Lavanya was sitting on their spot on the stairs, watching him play.

'Is this what you wanted to show me?' Shourya asked, opening the gate, his ancient guitar in one hand.

'Yes! Meet Toughy!' Lavanya's excitement was visible on her face.

'Tuffy? As in Salman Khan's dog in *Hum Aapke Hain Kaun*?'

'Kind of. Because Salman is the love of my life. But this puppy's name is *Tough-y*. Because he's a brave, tough boy. Aren't you a tough boy?' Lavanya bent down to pet the dog.

Shourya crouched down next to her and ran his fingers against Toughy's back, before nuzzling his ears. The puppy yelped happily and started running in circles around him.

'Yes, he likes doing that,' Lavanya said.

'Are you dog-sitting him?'

'No! He is *ours*. I got him for Mom. She was really scared at first, terrified; you should have been there. It was hilarious. But now, mere hours later, she absolutely adores him!'

'Who wouldn't? Look at him—his tiny legs wobbling and his cheeks drooping down so cutely.' Shourya caught Toughy in his arms and petted him, moving his index finger in circles on his forehead. His ears were facing front and he had a patch of white under his chin, running till his belly. 'So, excited about your first guitar lesson?' he asked Lavanya.

'Yup.'

'Shall we begin out here?' Shourya looked around. The sun was about to set, but it was still bright outside.

'No way. I do not want the world to witness my humiliation. We will sit in my room, where nobody can see us, and hopefully not hear us either.'

Shourya laughed. 'C'mon. You won't be that terrible.'

'How do you know?'

'Actually, I don't. You might really suck at it.'

'Haha,' Lavanya drawled, turning to Toughy. 'Come on in, boy! We gave him a bath this afternoon, and he has been running around ever since. He is only six weeks old; he must be so tired.'

'I don't think he wants to come in though.'

Toughy was busy playing with a sock, trying to rip it apart with his teeth.

'I need to buy him a ball and a nice fluffy box bed. I saw one online, but I want to go to the store and get it tomorrow. He has been living in such unfortunate conditions. He lost one of his legs to bully dogs when he was only a few days old. Poor kid.'

Shourya observed Lavanya as she watched Toughy play. Her face was free of worry lines, and for once her lips did not have the downward curve he had noticed on several occasions the last few days.

Lavanya picked Toughy up and gently pulled the balled sock out of his teeth. 'If you tear this too much, you are going to choke on it,' she whispered to him.

They brought the puppy inside with them. Mrs Suryavanshi was sitting near the living room window, reading the newspaper and sipping what looked like herbal tea. Mr Suryavanshi was watching the news.

'Suryavanshi family catching up on world affairs this evening?' Shourya remarked. Lavanya's parents looked up.

'Hello, Uncle!'

'Shourya,' Mr Suryavanshi took his outstretched hand. 'Come, sit. How have you been? Lavanya's mom told me you're in town. Your sister's wedding, huh?'

'Yes, Uncle. This weekend. All of you have to come. It'll be great to have you there.' Shourya always had trouble relaxing with Lavanya's father. He tended to become formal and polite. He had always only heard Lavanya's side of the story, and so whenever he met her father, he would try to act casual, as if he did not know Mr Suryavanshi's secret, but ended up coming off as stiff and proper.

'Of course we will be there, beta,' Mrs Suryavanshi chipped in. 'I bumped into your mother at the jeweller's the other day. She is so happy about the wedding.'

'Yes, she is. I think she started planning the day Shreela was born,' Shourya laughed. 'Although, in all probability, Shreela started planning from the womb itself.'

'Oh, I can imagine. I would be lying if I said I have not planned for Lavi's wedding myself!'

'Mom!' Lavanya, who had been hanging back with Toughy, shushed.

'It *is* true. Which mother does not plan her daughter's wedding? And it is not as if you are not a marriageable age now. We should start thinking about your future . . .'

'I cannot believe you are bringing up the marriage discussion again. Does it seem like the time and place?' Lavanya's nostrils flared in anger.

'Don't listen to your mom, Lavi. You are free to do what you want,' her father interjected.

There was silence. Shourya looked at Lavanya, who muttered through clenched teeth, 'I know.'

Mrs Suryavanshi got up just then and took Toughy off Lavanya's hands. 'I will put him down to sleep, but first, he needs to eat. This puppy needs to be fed so many times!'

Lavanya turned to Shourya and said, 'When you are done here, come up, okay?' She stomped away without waiting for a response.

Shourya stood rooted to the spot. *What just happened?* He chuckled nervously, trying to dissipate some of the tension in the room. 'Sensitive topic, wedding?'

'Oh, you know, girls these days,' Mrs Suryavanshi said quickly. 'You go on ahead. Lavi is very excited about learning to play the guitar.'

'I can't wait to see how this goes,' Shourya laughed.

When he went upstairs, Lavanya was sitting at the foot of her bed like she had the previous night.

'That was, umm . . . something?' Shourya said, standing at the door of Lavanya's room.

'I don't know what you mean.'

'You do.' He shut the door behind him and stood directly in front of her. 'What was that . . . *thing* with your father downstairs? Are you still punishing him?'

Lavanya did not speak. She did not even look at him.

'God!' Shourya exclaimed, the answer evident. His threw up his hands as he attempted to comprehend the meaning of this. The hours they had spent, sitting outside her house, preparing her to go in and face her life. The nights they had spent awake, talking on the phone, trying to get her mind off what was going on in her home. He had thought it was all in the past. But it was still just as real as it had been years ago.

'How . . .? How can you still be punishing him? Has it not been over a decade? True, there were cracks in your relationship, but what I saw downstairs was not mere cracks. Your relationship is still fucking broken.'

'Time is not as powerful as they tell you it is.' Lavanya looked up.

'Lavanya, we talked about this, didn't we? We said it was going to be easier once you were away for some time. You needed space and time, and we agreed that would help you.'

'It didn't.'

'I have trouble believing this. How can something that happened such a long time ago still affect you this way? You can't even look at him, or say more than two words to him? Do you talk to him at all?'

'No.' Lavanya's voice was flat.

'But why?'

'You *know* why! You know better than anyone!'

Shourya was silent. Lavanya's eyes were troubled. She looked much older than she had ten minutes ago. Shourya noticed the physical changes that had taken place in her over the course of years. Her eyes were the same, but looked different; her eyebrows were arched more neatly, prominently. Her cheeks had lost the slight roundness they had in her teenage years, making her cheekbones more pronounced. Her lips were curved downwards again. It seemed to be their natural resting state these days.

He kept looking at her, but Lavanya never looked back. She continued glaring at her fingernails.

After a while, Shourya decided to let it go. He had no other choice. He had known something was bothering her, and he had waited for her to bring it up, but if she did not want to, he was not going to force her. He saw no point in pursuing the topic if all she would do was ignore him and pick at her nails.

He hefted the guitar from his right to his left hand. 'Let's do this thing.'

8

Lavanya was reading her twelfth *Phantom* comic of the day when her phone buzzed. It was an email from Paxton-Stark-Meester reminding her that she had not shown up for work in weeks, and asking her to check in with them as soon as possible. *Another one of those.* She put her phone away and went back to reading *Phantom*

As a teenager, she had been obsessed with the Phantom. She used to find old comic books, dating back to the 1940s online and through other comic book enthusiasts and would read anything and everything that had the Phantom in it and was written by Lee Falk. Sometimes, the older comics, being classics, were priced beyond her buying power. She had promised herself she would hunt down and buy every last Lee Falk *Phantom* ever published once she started earning.

However, she had since forgotten about it. But after the guitar lesson with Shourya turned out to be such a disaster, she was intent on getting the second thing on her list ticked off as soon as possible. When her list told her she was supposed to find all these comics and read them, it turned out to be easier to achieve than she had expected. They were all available for purchase online at insanely low prices. She found fifteen books in the series she was looking for, and decided to devote an entire day to reading them.

She generally preferred reading books on digital platforms, but reading comic books on an iPad just felt wrong. She missed the delicate, worn-out pages infested by silverfish that threatened to turn to dust at her touch. She was not used to seeing the Phantom in vivid colours and HD. She remembered the images on the physical books being grainy.

It took her all afternoon to read twelve of them, and after that she simply could not bring herself to pick up comic number thirteen. She yawned and stretched her limbs. She was committed to her Lame Girl Dying Wish-List, and she kept telling herself she was having fun, but in truth the *Phantom* marathon had been nothing short of self-inflicted torture.

At least she had Toughy to keep her company. The poor puppy kept wiggling his tail in front of her, urging her to take him out to the lawn and play with him, but she had a wish list to complete. After a while, when he realized she was not going to play with him, he settled for lying down with his head on her lap.

Lavanya pulled out her list and put a tick against *Read all Lee Falk's Phantom comics*. On impulse, she also checked off *Learn to play the guitar*, scribbling 'tried' next to it. Her fingers were aching. Shourya had not gone easy on her. He had been angry about her refusal to discuss her situation with her father, and no matter how hard they tried to move past it, their mood was too sour to enjoy what they were doing.

He had asked her to cut her fingernails before they began, but she had stubbornly declined. Her nails, uneven and chipped from being gnawed on, had not performed well on the guitar strings. Her fingers would slip and she got minor cuts and bruises all evening. The terribly tuneless sound that came out of the guitar only made things worse. Nor did the fact that Shourya turned out to be a terrible teacher. He had picked 'Hotel California' for her first lesson, a song she had never heard before. He said it was a classic, the best acoustic guitar song of all time, but he never played more than the first few strings for her, before handing the guitar to her and asking her to play. And then he became frustrated when she could not. He had a problem with her nails, her posture, the way she held the guitar—everything.

In the end, they stopped speaking to each other, conversing exclusively through glares and sighs. She was relieved when, after an hour of torment, Shourya suggested they call it a day.

They had made a pact to help each other, but after the way the first item on the list had gone, Lavanya did not expect or even want any help from him. She had completed her second thing too. It did not matter that it had been no fun, as long as it was done.

Lavanya looked for something else in her list that she could do. There were a bunch of things she would not need any help with and could be done in a few hours. *Colour hair red. Get a tattoo. Belly-button piercing.*

She decided to start with hair colour.

Lavanya looked up the nearest salon and found one that was ten minutes' walk from the house. She made her way towards it, following the map closely. She remembered all the streets, but not what was on them any more. All the shops had changed, the buildings were not the same colour, even the smell was unfamiliar.

It was late afternoon, and stepping out of the house felt good. Artificial heating inside homes could not hold a candle to natural sunlight. It seemed a strange thought for her to have, one that would not even have occurred to her a month ago. After all, all her time was spent in artificially heated places and the only part of her body that ever came in direct contact with sunlight was the area below her sunglasses and above the collar of her suit.

She wondered if it was a side effect of *the news*.

It could be. Or maybe if she had cared to take a walk in the sunlight with nothing more urgent than getting her hair coloured, she might have experienced the wonders of sunlight before. Her mind as a corporate lawyer at PSM had constantly been cluttered with things she had to do and things Mr Cather told her she had done wrong.

When she reached the salon, she was surprised to find it was one of the big posh ones that charged twice the market rate and had hair dressers who looked down on you even though you're paying them to serve you. She pushed open the door tentatively and walked in.

A middle-aged female receptionist looked up, stretched her lips a mere three millimetres in what Lavanya assumed was a smile. 'HowmayIhelpyou?' All five words tripped over each other.

'Hey,' Lavanya hoped her smile was wider than three millimetres. 'I want to get my hair coloured.'

'Do you have an appointment?'

'No.'

The receptionist looked up at her in surprise. She asked, 'Have you met with one of our hair colour specialists for a consultation?'

'No. Is that a problem?' Two minutes in and Lavanya was already sick of being judged.

'Unless you consult with a specialist, we cannot be certain what shade is going to suit your skin colour and hairstyle. Also, we must determine the duration of leaving the bleach in and the strength of the developer to apply. We can show you a palette and decide the shade, and then advise you about highlights, lowlights, streaks, dip dyes and several ways we can go about colouring your hair. You will also be advised about after-colour care and precautions—'

'Is there someone here who can colour my hair?' Lavanya interrupted the receptionist.

'Ma'am, we do not recommend colouring your hair without a consultation first. We can offer you a package deal—hair colouring with one post-colour care treatment and two spa sessions. Consultation comes free of charge with the package.'

'Thanks, but I am not interested. For today, can I please just get my hair coloured?'

'I will have to insist. We are professionals, trained to cater to our clients' every need. We have a whole series of packages you can opt for. Hair colouring is just *one* step in the process of hair beautification, not the entire process.'

'But it's hardly invasive surgery, is it?' Lavanya's chuckle was met with a cold stare. 'Just hair colour, please?'

The receptionist did not attempt to hide her displeasure as she guided Lavanya inside.

'Thank you.'

And that was only the beginning. Her hair dresser, a girl in her early twenties named Ishi, was vehemently against colouring Lavanya's hair red. No matter how hard Lavanya tried to convince her that it was not about how she was going to look, that she did not care, it was just a tick mark on a list for her, Ishi did not give in.

'I can give you highlights in a lovely shade of burgundy. It's gonna look awesome in sunlight and it won't stand out too much under the yellow kinda light they have in restaurants and stuff, y'know?'

Lavanya told her she wanted red. Red, red, only red.

'I'm gonna have to bleach your hair for that. And then colour it red. And trust me, it's not classy at all. You don't wanna go around looking like you have a . . . What is that huge red bird called? Ostrich, I think . . . On your head, do ya?

In the end, Lavanya had to give up and let Ishi do as she pleased. It was strange how she had no control over the way the tasks on her lists were being completed.

~

Shourya did not sleep well that night. Lavanya had not called or texted him even once that day, and he had relapsed and visited Deepti's Facebook profile to check what she was doing. Always a mistake.

He saw a recent status update, where she had put up Johnny Depp's famous relationship quote about how if you love two people at the same time, you should go with the second because if you actually loved the first, you would not have fallen for the second.

Bullshit!

Was she trying to tell him that what they had had was not real? That *she* was the innocent one in the equation, because she could not stay faithful to one person? It was very easy to use general statements to justify one's actions, but nothing justified cheating. Even so, if quoting Johnny Depp was what she needed to do to be able to sleep at night, he was not going to take that away from her.

In fact, he did not want to have anything to do with her at all. It was habit that took him to her page, and boredom. Sometimes, when he tried to remember what being in a relationship with her had been like, he couldn't. There were so many images from after their break-up, so many incidents that crowded his head. He did not miss her. He only missed the thought of her.

When he woke up from his troubled sleep the next morning, he dialled Lavanya's number before he could convince himself not to give in.

'Hey,' she greeted.

'Okay, so, you know you need to apologize, right?' Shourya asked.

'*I* need to apologize? For what? Being a horrible teacher? And a mean and terrible friend and human being?'

'*Hey, hey, hey!* Only about fifty per cent of that is true about me. And it wasn't my fault, Suryavanshi. You were being an impossible pain in the ass. You know I cannot handle secrecy.'

'That's your problem, Kapoor,' Lavanya replied coldly.

'And that's not rude at all.'

'Argh, fine! But I am not going to apologize, and since I am not even mad at you any more I do not need you to apologize to me either.'

'Cool. So meet me at my place in half an hour?' Shourya suggested, only too happy to let the matter drop. One day without her had affected him more than he was willing to acknowledge.

'No. I am busy.'

'Doing what?'

'Getting a tattoo.' He could picture her smiling as she said it, but was not sure whether or not she was serious.

'*Really?*'

'Mm–hmm.'

'You're joking, Suryavanshi. You don't have the balls,' Shourya sat up on his bed. He had always planned to get inked some day too, but had never got around to it.

'Come and see. And then tell me if this looks like a joke to you.'

'Shit! Seriously? Where are you? It's ten in the morning!'

'I am leaving for the tattoo parlour. They also do piercings there. I'm gonna get myself one of those too,' Lavanya said. 'By the way, I also got my hair coloured yesterday. Since you weren't delivering on your end of the deal, I decided to take care of my list myself.'

Shourya sighed. 'If it makes you feel any better, I ruined my day without your supervision too.'

'What do you mean?' Lavanya sounded concerned.

'I went back to her Facebook—'

'NO! No. No, okay? Never do that. That is like the first rule, man. What on earth convinced you that stalking her would be a good idea? Are you stupid?'

'I guess I deserve that,' Shourya relented. Only Lavanya could insult him in a way that could make him smile. 'We clearly do need each other—'

'*I* don't need you,' Lavanya cut him off. 'I ticked two tasks off my list yesterday, without any help.'

'Okay, so that means the deal is off then, right?'

'Ye— *No!* I mean . . . well, you clearly need me. And I suppose I could use a hand now and then, even though I'm perfectly capable of handling this on my own, trust me. So, you know, whatever. We made a pact—let's keep it.'

'If putting it like that makes you happy, then so be it.' Shourya rolled his eyes, but he couldn't stop smiling. 'I'll pick you up.'

~

When Shourya pulled up in front of the tattoo parlour, he had doubts about getting inked here. The place looked dingy and dark, and not at all impressive from the outside.

'Are you sure this is the place?' he asked Lavanya.

'Ha! Chicken.'

'This does not look hygienic at all. We can look around for another place, can't we? What's so special about this one?'

'It's the one closest to my place on Google Maps,' Lavanya said simply.

'And that's it? I thought someone you know got inked here or you have some reasonably good testimony about the place at least. We can't get tattooed here just because it is closest to your place.'

'Why not? Watch me.'

Lavanya stepped out of the car before he could protest. Strands of her hair shone red under the morning sunlight. She had confessed that she was not pleased with it, but he thought her hair looked much nicer than the vivid red she had initially planned on getting done. By the time he parked and got out, she had already entered the parlour. He had no option but to follow.

'Let me see . . .' she was telling the guy at the reception. 'I want to get one word tattooed, here,' she pointed to her forearm. 'Can I see some font styles, please? Something in cursive, possibly?'

The place had dim lighting and red walls, one of which was covered entirely in pictures of tattoos the place claimed to have done, held in place by push pins. There were some exceedingly grotesque ones there too, which did not do anything to convince Shourya that this was not a bad idea.

There were numerous tattoos of skulls on the wall, but one of them was especially monstrous. One skull tattoo seemed to have three heads, and six eyes, positioned in a manner that made zero sense. But then, how could he expect sense from a man who got a giant skull inked on his back?

'Lavanya, we need to go,' he whispered in her ear.

'Aw, you leaving?' Lavanya asked loudly, looking at him straight in the eye. 'I thought you wanted to get one too.'

The man at the reception and the other three people in the room looked up at him, waiting for his reply. 'I think I will,' Shourya finally said.

'That's more like it. Have you decided what you are going to get?'

Shourya was a little annoyed at Lavanya's behaviour. She knew he was not comfortable with the shady place, but she wouldn't let him look up some other, better establishment. And she was enjoying putting him on spot, speaking loudly with everyone around listening in.

'Definitely not a skull,' he muttered. 'What are you getting?'

'I am going to get "always" written on the inside of my right wrist in this font.' She showed him a basic calligraphy font.

'Hmm. Book phrase? Isn't "always" a Harry Potter thing?'

Lavanya nodded. 'Severus Snape's eternal love for Lily Potter. And don't you dare make fun of me for getting a young adult fantasy book reference tattooed. I have not grown out of HP. I never will.'

'No, of course not. Potter's the best. This gives me an idea too.'

'Yeah?'

'Yeah.' Shourya said. 'Are you familiar with John Green's *Looking for Alaska*? There was this amazing concept in it.'

'Is this the same John Green who wrote *The Fault in Our Stars*? It is supposed to be really good, right? I have not read anything for the joy of reading since school, so I do not know much of the present reading trends.'

'Same guy. But I personally think *Looking for Alaska* is a much better book; leaves you with more to think about. You should read it.'

'Have you both decided your designs?' a young tattoo artist interrupted.

'Umm, I have,' Lavanya looked up at Shourya. 'You have decided too, right?'

'I'm not sure . . . How is it gonna look to people?' Shourya hesitated.

'Come on. If it means something to you, get it. Who cares what others think?'

'You can come this way,' the tattoo artist motioned Lavanya before turning to Shourya. 'Please go into that room. Michael will take care of you.'

'Thank you.' Shourya leaned in and whispered into Lavanya's ear, 'Are you sure, though? This place does not look very hygienic to me. It is okay if you don't want to do this. I mean, you don't *have* to, just because it's on your list. Or we could find a better place, maybe?'

'Relax,' Lavanya murmured, much to Shourya's relief was glad Lavanya was speaking softly too. 'It will be over before you know it. Don't think too much.'

'Is there nothing I can say to change your mind?'

Lavanya shook her head.

'Fine! It's decided then. We are getting Hepatitis or AIDS, or I don't know . . . some other kind of blood-borne infectious disease today. Let's face some needles,' Shourya patted Lavanya's back and nudged her towards her cubicle.

'At least we are in this together. See you on the other side!' he called, as he drew the curtain to the small room where Michael was supposed to take care of him.

9

Lavanya was steered into a dingy stall in a corner of the tattoo studio. The artist who would ink her introduced herself as Zia and asked her if she was ready. Lavanya did not respond in any way; no words, not even a nod. Zia did not seem to care. She started setting up the workstation.

Lavanya slumped into the reclining chair, her body curling inwards. It was as if her spine could not be bothered with keeping itself straight.

'You can relax. It is a relatively small tat. Not gonna take long.' Zia was wearing a translucent white tank top, her purple bra completely visible underneath, with neon green nylon shorts. Lavanya noticed how her entire right arm and whatever was visible of her chest was covered in one tattoo—a vibrant, red and gold snake coiled itself around her arm, all the way to her shoulder, its mouth open to reveal its fangs above Zia's chest.

For some reason, the snake's fang was pink in colour. Lavanya could not stop staring at it, not even when Zia caught her at it. A thin, sharp fang, almost like a needle.

Lavanya's eyes were drawn to the small machine that Zia was holding. Her fingers were around the coil of the tattoo gun, through which a thin needle emerged, inching closer to

Lavanya's skin. It was not one needle. There were five very fine needles disguised as one, but Lavanya was looking close enough to notice.

It was the only thing she could see. In that moment, it was the centre of the world. As she felt the first sweet prick of the needle, she was transported back to another time.

There was darkness. There were lights—red and blue and green—but they did not do anything to brighten up the room in the least. They did not need light anyway. They had enough of their own, inside.

Once they had white magic flowing through their veins, who needed light bulbs?

Her cheek was resting against something hard, and cold. Soon it did not feel cold any more. Whatever little warmth was left in her body was transferred to the cold tile, warming it. Her feet were freezing. She tried to pull them towards her body, but they refused to move. Not even an inch.

Her throat felt parched, her mouth dry. Except for the loud trance music blasting through the speakers, there was absolute silence. She had a funny feeling in her gut. Something terrible had happened.

She managed to push her body up, resting her palms flat against the floor. She had to sit like that for a minute, wait for her head to stop spinning, prepare her body for the next step—getting to her feet. It proved more difficult than she had expected. In the end, she settled for pushing herself back against the couch and resting her head on the worn edge. It was hard—the foam had given away and the woodwork was showing. Fortunately, comfort was the least of her concerns at that moment.

She looked around for her cell phone. Her head stayed still, only her eyes moved, scanning the room. She thought she saw the silver edge of her phone under an arm. With enormous effort, she crawled to it. The arm was large and hairy, just like the body it was attached to, its big belly rising and falling evenly, repeatedly. There was nothing lying around to cover it with.

She pushed the arm away, only to reveal a needle, some loose white powder, and a credit card. Those rectangular pieces of plastic had proved very useful that night. And also the needle. The silver of the needle glinted red, then blue, then green as the disco lights flashed. Red, blue, green. Repeat.

Lavanya jerked her arm away. The sweet pain shooting through her right arm did not cease. It was concentrated in one tiny point on her wrist. She gaped at it. A minuscule *A* sat there, red and throbbing.

'Is everything okay, ma'am?' Zia asked, looking at Lavanya with concern.

Lavanya's eyes shot up and met Zia's. 'Needle,' she muttered.

'Ah, it's no big deal. You've got to relax a tad. I'm going to be done before you know it.'

Zia pulled Lavanya's wrist back and tried to put it back in position, but Lavanya jerked it away again.

'Ma'am, it's okay. It won't hurt any more than the first letter, and that wasn't that bad, yeah?' Zia looked nervously at Lavanya, who shook her head. 'Did I do something wrong?'

Lavanya shot to her feet all of a sudden.

'Ma'am, please. Tell me if I did something wrong. My manager will kill me. He's always looking for an excuse to yell at me.' Zia's expression was terrified.

For a second, Lavanya almost sat back down. But her eyes fell on the needle again and she ran out of the stall, as if she could not leave fast enough. Her sneakers made a strange squeaky sound against the tiled floor.

'What's going on?' the man at the reception asked as Lavanya flew past him.

'ZIA! What did you do?' she heard him thunder.

Lavanya tried to turn back, to tell him that Zia had not done anything wrong, that it was the demons of her past that had chased her away. She could not be rescued any more, but she could help Zia keep her job. Even knowing that, her legs did not stop long enough for her to turn back.

She walked briskly towards Shourya's car. Too late, she realized she did not have the keys. She paced around the car, like a lunatic—round and round and round. She should have known better. *What was she thinking, getting a tattoo?* She had HIV. *HIV.* She was a threat to others; she could not risk getting her blood on a needle. She could infect someone if it wasn't sterilized properly. How could she have been so reckless? So thoughtless? She brought her wrist close to her eyes, looking at the tiny *A*. It was swollen, and red. The black ink was covered with her blood. Such an innocuous murder weapon.

Round and round and round.

HIV.

What if her immune system was not strong enough to heal the tattoo wound? What if it grew, and kept getting bigger till it covered her wrist, and then her hand and arm, slowly spreading across her body. What if she never got better again?

Round and round and round.

She needed answers. She could not keep running from it. What if the time she had wasted ignoring her condition made it too late for her? What if her condition kept worsening and there was nothing that could be done? *Doctor.* She needed to go to the doctor. She needed to get some tests done. She needed treatment. She chuckled. Who was she fooling? There was no cure.

Round and round and round.

Lavanya kept walking in circles around the car, her feet refusing to stop. She was getting dizzy, her legs were becoming wobbly, her armpits sticky. She pushed her hair back from her face angrily and was surprised to find it damp. Her cheeks were damp too.

Round and round and round.

She could not let Shourya anywhere near a needle. She had to stop him. She had to rush back in and drag him out with her. She had to tell him how stupid she was. What she had done.

Round and round and—*bump*.

Her knee collided with the car's bumper and a sharp pain shot through her leg. She buckled down to the ground, clutching her leg, her hands tightly wound around her knee, trying to block out the pain. Stupid. *Stupid, stupid, stupid.*

It was one thing to destroy your own life, but forcing the only friend you've ever had to participate in your stupid schemes, endangering his life? She was disgusted by herself. She craned her neck to look back at the tattoo parlour. Shourya had had his doubts about the place; he had asked her repeatedly if she was sure. If something were to happen to him . . .

Her head was bursting with *what ifs*. Her body had stopped trying to get back up. She sighed loudly, and bowed her head in defeat. Her eyes rested on her tattoo and she had the overwhelming urge to scratch it out. Her cheeks were still wet, and she did not know what to do about it.

Lavanya was living a lie. Keeping a secret that was killing her inside. She could not handle it, she now knew. It was too much. Every second that passed made her realize that she was one second closer to dying, and she was doing nothing to stall it. Nothing except pretending to be fine. Of 'protecting' those who loved her, as if the pain of her death would be easier than dealing with her sickness.

She was tired of pretending.

～

'What do you mean, she ran away?' Shourya asked the guy at the reception.

'She got up and ran away! I swear I did not do anything wrong. I asked her, but she did not say anything!' the young tattooist was saying animatedly.

'Where did she go?' Shourya went to the door to see if his car was still there; Lavanya couldn't have driven off since he had the keys. He pulled out his cell phone and dialled her number.

'Sir, sir . . . your bill,' the man at the reception called after him. 'And I will have to put madam's expense on your bill too?'

'Did she get her tattoo? You said she did not get it.' She was not taking his call. He dialled again.

'She got some of it—'

'Fine, put it on mine,' Shourya said. He paid the bill and rushed back to his car. Where could Lavanya have gone, without telling him? She was the one who had insisted they get this done. Her to-do list seemed important to her. It was unlike her to get up in the middle of it and run away without a clue. His car was sitting only a few yards away from the tattoo parlour. He looked around. Maybe she'd gone to a coffee place nearby to wait for him. Or maybe she'd gone back home, and was too ashamed of panicking and bolting to take his calls. She'd chickened out! He looked at his tattoo. It was still red and swollen, but it had turned out well. He had had his reservations about the place, but Michael turned out to be good at what he did. After the first few minutes, it was not bad at all.

On the inside of his left arm were the words 'great perhaps' in an old-school typewriter font. The main character in *Looking for Alaska* follows the words of the poet Francois Rabelais, who said, 'I go to see a Great Perhaps', and embarks on a pursuit of his own great perhaps. The idea of having a sense of purpose and connection to a grander cause had stayed with Shourya long after he'd finished reading the book.

Shourya could not wait to show off his tattoo to Lavanya. He walked around his car and . . .

'Lavanya?'

She was sitting on the pavement next to his SUV. She looked up, squinting in the sunlight, her face white like a ghost's. There were purple bags under her eyes, every vein visible under the thin translucent skin there. Her cheeks were red, the kind of red caused by an abrasion. To most people she would appear stressed and worn out, but not many would conclude tears. Except Shourya. He had seen her biting the inside of her lower lip far too many times to not know that she did that to keep her lips from trembling, a tell-tale sign of crying. It was obvious that she had been crying now. But there was also something in her eyes. Something . . . *more*.

Lavanya's eyes were squinted against the sunlight, but were gazing intently into Shourya's. Her lips were closed together, but her eyes were asking something of him, something he did not understand.

He dropped to his knees and crouched in front of her. 'What is it? What is wrong, Lavi?' He knew it wasn't about some stupid tattoo she'd chickened out of getting. She was hiding something from him, and if this was the condition her secret had left her in, he had to find out what it was.

'I want to go home.'

'Come on.' Shourya took both her hands in his and pulled her up with him. He deposited her in the passenger's seat and walked around the car to the driver's side. She would try to fight it, he knew. She never did give in easily. But this time he was not going to back down because he could see that she needed help.

He climbed into the car and slid the key into the ignition, but didn't turn it.

'Tell me,' he demanded softly.

Lavanya's eyes darted around the car, and she blinked several times before she turned towards him and met his eyes again.

'Seven years,' she said.

'What?' Shourya asked softly.

'That's how long I had not been home in. This is the first time I have come back since I left.'

No!

Shourya was thrown. He did not know how to respond at first. He tried to put all the pieces together. He had always known about her issues with her father and the troubles she faced with letting go of them. When he learned that she still had not been able to move on from what had happened with her father years ago, he was surprised. But now it made more sense. She had not been home in seven years—the trouble had not gone away. She had found it exactly as it was when she walked back in.

She could not move past it because she was still living in the past.

'It is the same . . . all still the same,' she muttered. 'Exactly how I left it. Only, Mom is older, and lonelier.'

'Why didn't you ever come back?'

'I could not . . . It wasn't like I didn't try. I called Mom sometimes and asked her how she was doing. I always made sure she was okay. But I could not come back here, Shourya, I could not. It was too hard and ugly and painful for me. '

'It did not need to be. I know you feel like you had to run away, Lavi, but you really did not. That was never the solution.' Shourya saw the pained expression on Lavanya's face and stopped.

'Why are you saying that now . . . now when I can do nothing to change it? To rub my mistakes in my face? To prove that I was wrong?'

'No. I'm sorry. I did not mean it in that sense.'

'I had to go. I *had* to. And at that time, I honestly believed that that was the only way I would ever be able to forget things and start over. I believed that it was the only way I would feel normal after . . . You have no idea what I went through.'

'I do, Lavi. Trust me, I do.' Shourya's tone was almost pleading. He could sense the agony she was in, and he wanted it to end.

'You don't!' Lavanya hissed.

Shourya reached out and held her hand. He felt it burn his skin for a second before she pulled away.

'We need to get you home. You have a fever.' Shourya started the car.

'No! You think it should have been easy for me. To forget about it, to forgive him and move on. Turn a new leaf, begin a new chapter, or whatever fancy name you want to give it. But it is not as simple as that. Once you've seen your father . . . naked in your science teacher's bedroom . . . *You* try to live with something like that, and tell me if it is easy!' Lavanya said heatedly, tears flowing down her cheeks. 'Nobody had any respect for me. I was the butt of all jokes. He was the one having an affair, but I became the school slut.'

Shourya could see what the conversation was doing to Lavanya, but he could not stay quiet. He had to speak up. 'I never said it was easy. But running away was never the solution. What's changed now that you've come back so many years later, other than the fact that everyone is almost a decade older? You're picking up from where you left off. If anything, judging by that night when I was over, things have only become more awkward.'

'Of course they have! He never even apologized!'

'How could he? Have you even given him the chance to speak to you? How is he supposed to say anything to you, when you don't talk to him at all? Have you ever stopped being angry with him long enough to consider how tough it must be for him?'

'*Him?*' Lavanya shrieked. 'What do you care about him? Why are you always taking his side?'

'Lavanya! Be reasonable. I did not say I was taking his side, I am just trying to see how it must have been for him. One mistake and that has defined the way his daughter is going to treat him for the rest of his life.'

'It was not a small mistake, Shourya!' Lavanya snapped. 'You know how tough it became for me to even go to school.'

'I know. And I understand what you went through. I was there through most of it, and I am here now. You know that.' Shourya tried to hold her hand again, and this time, she let him. 'Listen,' he continued after a pause, 'you just got here. It took you long enough, but the fact that you were able to come here shows that you are stronger than you give yourself credit for. Give it time.'

'Weren't seven years enough?' she sighed, resting her back against the car seat and closing her eyes.

Shourya reached out and touched her cheek. 'Seven years when you weren't here. Now you are, and it's only been, what, seven days?'

'It's too difficult, Shourya.'

Shourya could see her closed eyelids pressed in deep pain. Her breathing was slow and deliberate. He did not want to argue with her any more. She was running a fever and becoming groggy—she clearly needed rest. 'Yes, it is,' he said. 'But it's going to be okay soon.'

He made her fasten her seatbelt and drove her back home. Her eyes were closed the entire time.

10

Lavanya took the long way around the huge lawn in front of All India Institute of Medical Sciences (AIIMS). She walked briskly, intently, wasting no time. Even though it had been a long time since she had lived in Delhi, she feared being spotted in the hospital. It was the last thing she needed.

She had stayed up all night, reading up on the Internet, which was overflowing with countless resources for people infected with HIV. The websites she found were very . . . kind. She Googled 'what happens if i am tested hiv positive' and read from the first ten sites that were listed in the search results. After four hours of reading through government and healthcare sites, she had a sense of what the next steps for her would probably be.

But first and foremost, the thought that gave her a flicker of hope was reading 'Being HIV positive is no longer a virtual death sentence' on a webpage. She had read that one phrase repeatedly, feeling marginally better each time. It motivated her to research her disease as extensively as she could. There were articles explaining how HIV takes time to progress till AIDS and how, when controlled through medication and treatment plans, some patients have lived long lives.

As soon as it was light outside, Lavanya pushed her comforter away and got out of bed. Toughy stretched once and then curled up again, burrowing deeper into the mattress. She showered quickly, dressed and left for AIIMS quietly.

She should have done this weeks ago, when she had first found out. Reading through the articles, she became hopeful that she would be okay, that her condition was not as bad as she had imagined, that there was still a chance for her.

There was a man at the reception, and many people sitting in the waiting area. Lavanya had not made an appointment beforehand, so she had to wait for her turn. She took a seat on one of the shiny metal benches lined against the hospital wall. It was still early in the morning, but the waiting area was packed. She tried not to look at anybody or anything except her hands resting on her lap, picking at her fingernails. She could hear children crying and mothers trying to soothe them. The boy sitting next to her did not have an arm. Another had a bandage on his right eye.

Lavanya looked up more information on her phone just so she would not have to see what other patients and their families were doing. It was all she could do to stay calm and not bolt from the hospital without consulting a doctor.

She got a call from Shourya, which she quickly rejected. She was not ready for it; she had not even thought of a cover up.

Instead, she sent him a text. *Hi. Morning.*

He texted back. *Good morning. What's up?*

Lavanya dodged his question. *How come you are up so early? It is not even 9.*

Wedding's tomorrow. Sleep prohibited.

Sounds lovely.

How are you? Feel better?

Fever is all gone. Much better.

'Lavanya Suryavanshi!' A short man with a moustache peeked into the waiting area and called.

Lavanya kept looking into her phone.

The orderly looked around and when nobody responded, he called again, 'LAVANYA SURYAVANSHI!'

She stood up. 'That's me.'

'Come this way.'

Lavanya followed him to the doctor's office in silence. She had her blood report with her, tucked away safely in the deep inside pocket of her jacket. She had been very careful with it, lest someone accidentally find it.

The orderly knocked on the door before pushing it open and holding it for her. Lavanya's legs had never felt so weak in her life. They were a constant betrayer. Every time she was faced with a challenge, they were the first to give up. Even now they were shaking. She willed them to stop quaking long enough for her to make it to the doctor's desk with some dignity.

Dr Meera Shah had many years' experience in the field of HIV and AIDS. According to the website Lavanya had checked, Dr Shah was forty-seven years old, but in person she looked much younger. She wore a long white coat over a petite frame, her frizzy hair gathered in a bun at the nape of her neck. She looked over her spectacles to greet Lavanya.

'Ms Suryavanshi, please take a seat.'

Lavanya smiled nervously and sat down opposite to the doctor. 'Hi.'

'How may I help you? I hear you requested me especially?'

'Yes, Doctor.' Even sitting down, Lavanya's legs would not stop shaking. She pressed her feet hard against the floor in an attempt to curb the jolts. 'I read several testimonials and recommendations of your work on the Internet. That is why I wanted to meet with you,' Lavanya blurted out.

'That's nice to know.' Dr Shah smiled.

Lavanya pulled out her blood report, carefully unfolded it and straightened out the creases. Her hand trembled slightly as she handed over the document to the doctor. She zipped her jacket back up and stared at her fingernails.

There was silence for a minute.

'Do you know what this means, Lavanya?' she heard Dr Shah ask.

Her nails were ugly. They were brittle and uneven and discoloured.

'This report is a month old. How much do you know? Lavanya?'

Lavanya shook her head. 'Nothing.'

'Have you met with an HIV/AIDS specialist?' Dr Shah questioned.

Lavanya marshalled what little courage she had and looked up. 'I have not met with anyone, Doctor. I have known that I am HIV positive for three weeks, but I have not been able to meet anyone about it since. So, no, I do not know anything about it, other than that I have it.'

'Okay. That's an understandable response. Why don't you tell me whatever you know, first? Then I will guide you through the next steps.'

Lavanya tore off a part of her nail with another nail. 'I got this standard test done to validate me to donate blood at a drive. That's how I found out. That's . . . that's all I know. I have not seen a doctor before this, so I do not know anything more.'

'What about how you got it, and when? Would you have an idea?'

'Needle. A few months ago. Two, or three, I guess.'

Dr Shah held Lavanya's gaze. 'That would mean you are out of your infection phase. Do you remember having a fever, or a flu-like condition developing around that time?'

'No, I do not think so.' Lavanya was getting less and less agitated as she talked to Dr Shah about it.

'Well, all right. We will need to conduct a few tests to assess the situation accurately. But the first course of business—I should explain to you what being HIV positive means.'

'Okay,' Lavanya whispered.

'When a person is infected by the Human Immunodeficiency Virus, they go through an acute infection phase. Some experience a flu-like condition, which they mistake for a viral fever. Others do not have it at all. After this first phase, the patient moves into the second phase, which is clinical latency. The virus reproduces inside the patient's body, the rate of which can vary from person to person, but is usually very low. Are you with me till now?'

Dr Shah was observing Lavanya closely, which made Lavanya uncomfortable. But then, she hadn't expected this to be easy.

'Yes, Doctor. I read about it last night. After the clinical latency, we get to AIDS.'

'Right. It is when the patient's CD4 cells fall below a certain level—200 cells per millimetre cube—that's when the patient is considered to have progressed to AIDS. But,' Dr Shah paused, and Lavanya looked up at her, 'if you are sure you got infected two or three months ago, I can say that you have passed your infection phase and are in latency. You did the right thing by coming to us; early detection is key. What we do now, in this phase, is what defines the course your life takes from here.'

'How long will I live?' The words were out before Lavanya knew it.

'I cannot say anything until we perform the tests. We have to evaluate how your immune system is working, the rate at which the virus is progressing and your overall health. That's when we decide what course of treatment is your best fit—'

'Yes, but, you must be able to estimate, right? I read that people can live full, long lives with HIV and never have it progress till AIDS. And that even if it is left completely untreated, the latency period can last as long as ten years and even after that AIDS can take three more years to kill you!'

'Ms Suryavanshi, Lavanya, we have to conduct these tests on you and only then can I discuss this with you further.'

'Yes, yes, of course . . . I am not saying we should not perform tests. We will do that, of course, we must . . .' Lavanya rattled on. 'But I . . . I just want a rough estimate, you see. If it's only been three months tops, and without treatment I could go on for thirteen years, then with treatment I have . . . what? At least fifteen? Is that how it works?'

'That is not the way we—' Dr Shah started saying something but Lavanya interrupted.

'Or are there side effects of the treatment that can work *against* me and *reduce* my lifespan? Does that happen? And what about injuries? If I get hurt, is it going to keep getting worse till I die? Will it never heal, because the virus is going to kill my immune system? Also, what about my quality of life? Will I have to be very careful, all the time? Will I have to be admitted in a hospital all my life, or can I lead a normal life? And what about sex—if I have protected sex, might I still transmit my virus? Can I never have sex then?'

Dr Shah pushed back her chair and got up. It was the scraping of the wood against the floor that made Lavanya pause and look up. Dr Shah walked around her desk and sat in the chair next to Lavanya.

'Lavanya, I know this must be very confusing and frightening. I wish I could have told you we have only the best case scenario ahead of us, but unless I see those reports, I cannot say anything. Textbook knowledge can only take us so far. I know it must help you to read about it online and there are some forums that I can suggest, which you could benefit from. But *first*,' she put additional emphasis on the word, 'we *must* perform the tests. That is of prime importance.'

'I understand,' Lavanya said quietly. It was as if the energy that had kept her going all this while had disappeared.

'I can see that you have several questions and your head must be bursting with many more. I will be able to answer them once I have a better sense of your case. Let me write down the tests. We can get them done at the hospital immediately. Then once we have the reports, we can talk more?'

Dr Shah took a pen from the red–and–white capsule-shaped pen stand on her desk and wrote down the tests.

'Thank you, Doctor,' Lavanya said and got up.

'Sure. I will inform you once we have the results and then we can meet and discuss everything.' Dr Shah offered her hand with a smile.

Lavanya shook her hand, but could not smile.

~

'Shreela!' Shourya called. 'Has anyone seen her?' he asked the room in general. There were at least thirty people in the living room just then. Although quite large, the room was not designed to accommodate that many people at once. Shourya wondered, not for the first time, if he should have taken Shreela's side and had a smaller wedding.

'Excuse me? Aren't you Shreela's friend?' Shourya asked a tall girl in a fancy sari whom he had seen with Shreela earlier that evening. 'Do you know where she is? Is she ready yet?'

The girl paused in her tracks and took a second to blush, before saying, 'Yes, she is in your parents' room. She was looking for you too.'

'Was she? Thanks.' Shourya made his way upstairs. The baraat was about to arrive and he could not believe that no one was prepared to receive it.

He knocked on the door to his parents' room and walked in. Shreela was sitting on the bed with her head on their father's shoulder, weeping openly. Their mother was standing next to the dressing table, looking at them with tears in her eyes.

'Wow. I know, wedding time, emotional time, our little darling isn't going to be here with us tomorrow, and it's all very sad and beautiful and we would like to take a minute and cry about it, but can we get on with the wedding first?' Shourya said.

'Ugh, you're so mean!' Shreela dabbed at her face carefully with a tissue and sniffed.

'You're only making it worse. Mom, can you ask someone to get the beautician back in; I think I saw her around somewhere? And Dad, I had expected this from the women, but you too? The baraat will be here any minute. You're the one person who absolutely has to be there to greet the guests.'

'Yes. Yes,' his father shot to his feet. He kissed Shreela on the forehead and ran his hand over her hair.

'Now you're messing up her hair! Now they're going to need another hour to fix it. Dammit! Mom, also get the hair guy here, please?'

Both their parents left in a hurry, leaving Shourya alone with Shreela. She continued to sniff softly. Her dupatta was pinned to her right shoulder and draped across her body. It was red and had tiny sequins all over it that glittered at the slightest movement. Had Shourya not expected to see her as a bride, he would not have recognized his baby sister. Her eyes were lined with thick black liner and her lipstick was the brightest shade of red. The necklace she was wearing was at least three inches wide and her earrings four inches long.

Shreela secured the thin straps of her shiny sandals and stood up.

'Are you okay? Isn't all this weighing you down?' Shourya asked. Her lehenga was a very light shade of peach, and was hand-embroidered in red all over. Teamed with the dupatta and her jewellery, Shreela was balancing a fair amount of weight on five-inch heels.

'I'm okay,' she said and walked to the dressing table. She sat down on the stool in front of the mirror and attempted to fix her hair.

'You sure?' Shourya asked.

'Yes. I have been training for this day since forever. It is going to be perfect.'

Her voice was flat and dull. For someone who had trained for her wedding day 'since forever' and planned for it for months, she did not seem quite as excited.

Shourya needed to join his father at the main gate to receive the groom.. He could hear the band music getting louder as the baraat drew near. It was the silence he was receiving from Shreela that scared him.

He went and stood behind her. Watching her face closely in the mirror, he asked, 'Nervous?'

She continued fiddling with her hair, which only made it worse. She inadvertently pulled out several strands from her bun, which fell in front of her face. She pushed them away angrily, muttering, 'This . . . *stupid* . . . thing.'

'Leave it alone,' Shourya chuckled. 'Mom is bringing your make-up people upstairs.'

Shreela let her hands fall into her lap and looked up at Shourya in the mirror. 'Are you going to miss me when I'm gone?'

'Not really. No more than I already do. Whether you live here or with Manav doesn't matter to me, distance-wise; I'll still be thousands of miles away,' Shourya said, and immediately regretted it. 'But of course, I will miss you! Is that even a question?'

'You are always so mean to me.'

'Older brothers are supposed to be.'

'Even on their younger sister's wedding day?' Shreela's eyes were larger than ever as she waited for Shourya's response.

'Don't make that face! I am not being mean to you. I've been trying my damnedest to give you your dream wedding. Making sure everything is perfect. Except how will it be perfect if I am here when your groom and the rest of his baraat are out there waiting for me to greet them and I am in here chatting with you?'

'That's *all* you care about!' Shreela sniffed angrily.

'I thought that's what *you* wanted! Isn't that why you've been after my life to take care of every last detail since I got here?' Shourya was exasperated.

'Ugh, fine, go.'

'Thank you! We will talk about this later. I know you must be anxious and scared, but like you said, you've been training for this all your life. You're going to be great.'

Shourya was at the door when he turned around, 'Wait, aren't you going to be cold? Do you want a shawl or—'

'No!' Shreela stood up hastily and examined herself in the mirror. Inches and inches of midriff were exposed between her backless blouse and the top of the lehenga. 'I dieted and did crunches every day for *three* months to get this stomach. This is my day, I'm showing off!'

And with that, Shourya knew Shreela was okay.

He rushed to the front gate just in time to see Manav dismount from the horse he was riding. He was wearing a sherwani in beige and red, very similar to Shreela's lehenga. The glitter around Shourya made him dizzy. Everyone—

women *and men*—was wearing brightly coloured clothes embellished with sequins or stone work or embroidery.

Shourya had chosen the most subtle sherwani he could find at the store before his mother and sister could reject it as being too simple. His mother had ulterior motives. 'You're the bride's single older brother. There are going to be lot of eyes on you. I bet we will get at least ten rishtas for you in the week after the wedding.' Shourya was just glad his clothes did not have colourful stones on them.

~

Barring one awkward moment when one of the baraatis felt offended because he wasn't welcomed with a garland, the wedding went by smoothly. Shourya was on his toes all night long, prepared to troubleshoot, come what may.

Lavanya and her parents arrived shortly after the baraat and she stayed by Shourya's side for the remainder of the night. As the wedding ceremony proceeded, Shourya was asked to tie a knot, binding Shreela's and Manav's dupattas together, before the seven pheras around the fire commenced.

Shourya took a seat directly in front of Shreela and Manav and watched as they performed the wedding rituals together. Manav kept stealing looks at her, and Shreela blushed every time that happened. His little sister was all grown up and looking beautiful on her wedding day.

Shourya fought back tears, nearly losing control until he felt Lavanya's hand clutching his.

11

When Lavanya's head touched the pillow, she felt herself finally relax, both mentally and physically. She had had a headache all night, which had worsened because of the loud wedding music. She feared it had to do something to do with her illness. Or it could just be a migraine. She had over-exerted herself on the dance floor along with all of Shreela's friends. When they had first requested Lavanya to join them, she had been naïve enough to think they would go away if she politely declined their invitation. But that hadn't deterred them; they had dragged her on to the dance floor despite her protests. The party had really got going when Shourya and the groom's friends had jumped in. Lavanya did not remember the last time she had danced to Hindi and Punjabi songs that were loud, rowdy and, quite frankly, disrespectful to women at times. The dancing had continued for hours and it wasn't until nearly all the guests had left and the DJ asked to wrap up that they realized what time it was.

'Wow . . .' Lavanya sighed.

'I know!' Shourya groaned as he lay down next to her on the bed. His house was crawling with relatives from all around the country and friends that were staying over the night for Shreela's bidaayi in the morning. Shourya had refused to let Lavanya go.

'So glad your mom kept this room locked for you. Cannot imagine being around so many people any longer,' Lavanya mumbled sleepily.

'Mmm.'

'It was fun, right?'

'Mmm-hmm.'

'I have never danced so much before.'

There was no response from Shourya. She turned on her side and faced him. He was lying on his back with his eyes closed. Lavanya poked his arm. He did not stir. She poked him again. Nothing. Lavanya propped herself up on an elbow and observed him. His chest was rising and falling evenly, his eyes were shut and his face relaxed. He must have been exhausted, to fall asleep as soon as he lay down. Lavanya poked his arm repeatedly till he woke up, startled.

'Huh? What . . . *what*?' he blurted.

'I have never danced so much before.' Lavanya smiled.

'I was sleeping,' Shourya said, feeling disgruntled.

'Were you?' Lavanya feigned ignorance. 'I thought you wanted to talk to me. If you wanted to sleep, why did you ask me to hang back?'

'Because I wanted you around.' Shourya sat up against the head rest grudgingly and rubbed his eyes. 'My neck hurts.'

'My entire body hurts.'

'Why does your body hurt? You didn't do anything, except dance a little. I've been busting my ass all day every day for two weeks.'

'Please. It was hardly *little*. But I have to give it to you— you did a great job with the wedding arrangements. Not a single flower out of place.' Lavanya stifled a yawn as she sat up in front of Shourya.

'Actually, there were some flowers out of place,' Shourya confided. 'Manav's father's cousin's friend felt disrespected because he wasn't greeted with a garland like the rest of the baraatis. We over-prepared for everything. We were told to arrange to receive sixty baraatis. I ordered a hundred garlands, and we were still one short!'

Lavanya chuckled. 'Don't beat yourself up about it. He sounds like someone creating a nuisance just *because*. Besides, I don't understand why garlands would matter to someone. They all take them off in about five seconds.'

'I don't know. They look for "respect" in these things or whatever.'

'I guess.'

Shourya's eyes were red, and sad. Seeing him watch as Shreela and Manav got married, she could see how it had affected him. She had seen his jaw clench and stay that way till the time it was over. He had not looked at Lavanya the entire time, but he hadn't let go of her hand either.

'Are you okay?' she asked. 'You look shaken up.'

Shourya's eyes met hers. 'I'm okay, I'm okay. Only . . . I was so caught up with the preparations that . . . when I had time to sit down and *see* . . .'

'Do you think they are not going to be happy . . .?'

'No, no, of course not. They adore each other. They *are* kids, but they'll figure it out. Manav has a lot of work cut out for him.' Shourya laughed.

'He seems so much in love with Shreela. Did you see how he kept whispering something in her ear? They were giggling so much! I think the priest even got offended at one point.' Lavanya ran her fingers over the edge of Shourya's sherwani. It was a dark shade of maroon that shone under the light. 'Is this silk?'

'I think so. Listen, can we sleep now? I am exhausted.'

'It is already. Shreela's bidaayi is in an hour. Will you be able to wake up if you go to sleep now?' Lavanya asked. A portion of his neck was exposed just above the collar of his sherwani. The maroon silk next to his skin offered a contrast she could not tear her eyes away from.

'I guess it's better to stay up till the bidaayi. I'm going to sleep for ten hours after she leaves and it's finally over.'

'Makes sense.' She nodded, still staring at his neck.

Shourya stretched, his joints cracking. 'How do you guys handle the cold in these clothes? Half of your body is exposed.' He pointed to her stomach.

'Stop looking at my exposed body.'

'Then stop showing it!'

'I'm wearing a sari to a wedding. That is what I am expected to do. And saris expose tummies. You're the one staring!' Lavanya felt her ears get warm. She hoped they were not turning red as well.

'Ah, you don't have anything to hide. You have a nice tummy.'

'Don't call it a tummy. That makes it sound fat.'

'I said tummy because you said tummy,' Shourya grinned.

'I said tummy because the word is asexual. Reminds me of cute little girls.'

'Why were you thinking about cute little girls' tummies?'

'I wasn't!' Lavanya glared at Shourya. '*God!* Will you stop? Women don't get affected by the cold weather once they are all dressed up. Simple as that.'

'Okay. I was just asking.' Shourya raised his hands in surrender.

Lavanya tried to find something other than her stomach to talk about. Sitting down was not the best position for stomachs to look flat and she could not keep it sucked in much longer. She rearranged the pallu of her sari over herself to hide whatever little she could.

'What's new with you? Anything on the ex-girlfriend front?' she asked, looking to change the topic.

'As a matter of fact, she called.' Shourya was no longer looking at Lavanya.

'What? Why didn't you tell me? We are supposed to talk about every new development.'

'I was trying not to think about it.'

'Did you take her call?'

'Yes.' Shourya's voice was low.

'And? What did she want?'

Shourya was quiet for a few minutes, then he looked up at Lavanya. 'She wants us to get back together. She said Avik took her away on a cruise and proposed to her and she panicked. She did not know what else to do but say yes, so she did. She thought that if she did not say yes right away, there would be another big fight between them. She said she thinks Avik is insecure and doesn't trust her.'

'I think Avik is right to be insecure when it comes to her. She agreed to marry him, took the ring, and then she is calling you to get back together? Not someone *anyone* should trust.'

Shourya started to say something. 'I—'

'*Including* you.'

'She is not that kind of a person—'

'Shourya Kapoor, are you really thinking about taking her back?' Lavanya could not believe what she was hearing.

'I have known her for so many years, Lavanya. It is not that simple. I know the kind of person she is. She messed up and she is confused and scared and . . . I don't know. She is just trying to figure things out.'

'I don't believe this! How can you let her get under your skin like this? You are still taking her side, as if she's never wronged you.' Lavanya was furious at him. He knew what Deepti could do to him—he had already been through it once. How could he even think of letting her do that to him again?

'I am not taking her side. I am just saying that everybody makes mistakes. She was confused and . . . When you've known someone for as long as I knew Deepti, you can't judge them based on any one thing they did. She did something horrible to me, but she also did so many good things. She was with me for so long. We've been through a lot together.'

'I know that. I get that. You were together for six years, you must have been very close. She must have done a lot of good things for you, but so did you for her, right? And in the end none of it mattered to her.'

'You can't judge her like this!' Shourya cried.

'I can and I will. You obviously cannot think clearly when it comes to her, so someone has to do it for you.'

'You only want to see the bad in her. She was going through something she did not understand. It was a new country, we had new friends, new lives. She made a mistake . . .'

Lavanya sighed. 'Fine, you're right, I have blinkers on when it comes to her, I only want to see what she did wrong. But that's because you're the one I care about. She means nothing to me. It is *not* my job to worry about her or what she was going through then or what she wants now. I only care about what you want. And that is what we need to figure out.'

Shourya held his face in his hands, resting his elbows on his knees while he sat in front of Lavanya, who refused to let up. He could see where she was coming from; she was only trying to protect him, but he could not help but feel angry at her too. He had been trying not to bring it up since they'd met in the grocery store. It had happened years ago, there was no point in bringing it up.

'She was with me through the hardest years of my life.'

'Shourya, look at the big picture. Look at what happened in the end and then decide. Do you want to make yourself go through all that again?' Lavanya asked. She was sitting in front of him, Indian style, leaning towards him and gesturing wildly as if she was talking to a crazy person.

As if he was the one who didn't understand.

'She was there when I didn't know what I wanted to do with my life. Up until then, I'd had a relatively easy life, no big challenges or decisions to take. When I got out of school, I joined the best engineering college that I got accepted to. But what next? I had no plans. She encouraged me to do whatever I wanted; she was confident that I would succeed. She shared my dream . . . We took the journey together. We worked for it together and we reached it,' Shourya said quietly.

'But you didn't! She held you back. *Harvard* was your dream, not Berkeley!'

'UCB was amazing. It was good for me. Everything I know, I learned there.'

'Yes, I am sure it was great. But you had to *settle* for it, only because she did not get into Harvard.'

Shourya could see Lavanya getting more and more agitated.

'It was a stupid childish wish, not a real dream. UCB gave me everything Harvard offered—'

'*You told me Harvard was your dream.* Just last week, you told me. What changed?'

'I guess I only wanted to focus on what I gave up for Deepti so I could hate her more. I did not want to think of all the things I got because of her, with her. Now when I think about it, I can't help but wonder if my *dream* of going to Harvard really mattered to me.'

'Shourya, I don't understand.' Lavanya spoke softly. She reached out and took both of Shourya's hands in hers.

Shourya looked at their hands—hers, small and pale and cold, holding his. 'Fourteen years, Lavanya. From the day I met you in kindergarten, till the day we left school—we were together every day. I was used to having you around all the time. But you were obsessed with Harvard; you couldn't wait to finish school and run off there. And then all you could think of was getting away from your father and the people in school who bullied you.'

'Shourya, don't do this,' Lavanya said in a quiet voice.

'You can't run away from this, Lavanya. Running away is your solution to everything, but I won't let you. Not this time.'

Lavanya pulled her hands back and moved away from him.

'I was there too,' Shourya continued. 'I was with you, *all the fucking time*, never letting anyone so much as pass a comment on you. I tried to protect you from them as much as I could. I know it was tough. All our classmates teaming up against you, making fun of you because of your father's relationship with Mrs Dey . . . I know how hard it was for you . . . but I was there, dammit!'

Lavanya nodded.

'I went through what you went through. Every snide remark that reached your ears reached mine too. And believe it or not, it hurt me just as much as it did you. But you were so caught up in your own pain that you didn't see any of that, did you? You were hell-bent on getting out of there and never looking back. On leaving everything and everyone behind and starting over. I was just another casualty,' Shourya shrugged, remembering the time she'd told him that she got a call from Harvard.

'*Don't say that!*' Lavanya protested.

'You were so happy. I bet you didn't think of me even once. I had promised myself I wouldn't hold you back, but I slipped once, didn't I? Do you remember? When we were shopping for those big bags you needed to take to the US? I could see it happening in front of my eyes. For the first time, I realized that it was time. You were going. I had to stop you. I begged you to stop. I didn't know how to function without you. For as long as I could remember, I had always had you around. You were my best friend, brother, sister, constant companion—everything. I couldn't imagine living without you.'

Shourya moved closer to Lavanya. He held her chin and made her look at him. 'You knew how I felt about you . . . and you asked me not to say it. You told me to keep it to myself, if I cared about you, and you told me to let you go because that was the only thing that could make you happy. That you would die if you had to live here for one more day.'

Shourya got up. He could not look at her any more. She was crying. He felt like such a heel for bringing up something that happened such a long time ago and blaming her for it, when he had seen first-hand what it had been like for her. She had only been trying to find a way to exist without going through torture every day. Even when school was finally over, she had to live with her father and as soon as she saw him, everything came flooding back to her. Keeping it a secret from her mother had been the hardest thing she'd ever done. The whole school knew, and openly ridiculed her, but it fell on Lavanya to look after her mother. She did not know whether to tell her or not. In the end, she could not do it. Everyone knew her family was dysfunctional, broken, but she could not bring herself to actually break it.

'I did not mean to hurt you the way I did . . . Shourya . . .' her voice trembled.

'I know. I know,' Shourya nodded, moving away. He started pacing the floor. 'But you did. I know you were only seventeen and you had a lot to deal with. But I was seventeen too! And when I lost you . . . You said we would keep in touch, that we would talk all the time,' he said, barely able to keep the accusation out of his tone. 'It took you a week to give me your number! And afterwards you never answered my calls or texts. You cut me off completely. Do you know what I went through? Do you have any idea? You were alone in a foreign country, you knew no one there, and you wouldn't talk to me or your parents—I was worried sick about you.'

'But I told you not to worry. I was okay. I took care of myself.'

'Yes, but *I* didn't know that! I missed you terribly. All I could think of was finding a way to be with you. Getting into Harvard seemed the best way to do that. I hadn't taken any entrance exams or anything—I didn't even know what course I would study. When the engineering entrance results came out, Dad made me join college. That was when I started planning for a master's at Harvard. It was a misguided plan from the very beginning.' Shourya looked up and released a long breath. 'And then I met Deepti. I made the same mistake that I'd made with you; I made her my life. But I wasn't like you. I could not leave her behind when college ended. She had not planned for her future after graduating, so I gave her a plan.'

Shourya stopped walking and stood in front of Lavanya, who was sobbing softly into her hands, facing away from him.

'You do not get to make my decisions when it comes to Deepti. You're no better than her. Both of you did the same thing to me. You could call what she did worse, you could use the words *cheating* and *betraying* and *rejecting*, but it felt the same to me. You chose something else over me too. You betrayed me too. I felt abandoned and rejected by both of you, and it was heart-breaking for me both times, but with her, at least I had some experience.'

'I'm sorry. I'm so sorry . . .' Lavanya's arms were wrapped tightly around her body. It was as if she was holding herself together lest she shatter into a million pieces. Her head was bowed, her hair falling around her face, hiding it from view.

Shourya looked away from her. He could not bear knowing he was the reason she was in so much pain. Yet the words came out before he could stop them. 'At least she came back. At least she loved me back. You . . . you wouldn't even have talked to me again had I not come to meet you that day at the grocery store. When we met, it was as if nothing had ever gone wrong between us. We picked up right where we had left off. But what happens when this vacation is over? Two more weeks and then you'll return to your life and I to mine. Will I ever hear from you again? You keep telling me that I should not trust Deepti. Then tell me: Whom to trust? You? You, with your secrets and running away. All you have ever thought about is yourself. At least Deepti realizes what she did. If I can't trust her, then I should never trust you. You are ten times worse . . . you hurt me ten times more.'

12

Lavanya had nothing to say in her defence. She did not even try to control the sobs that were shaking her body and the tears that dampened her sari. She scratched her face, trying to wipe it with the pallu of her sari, which was heavily embellished with sequins. She gave up and let the tears flow freely down her face.

This was Shourya. She did not need to put up a front for him. If it affected her, she could show him. She did not have to pretend to be strong with him. It was liberating. However, it did not help her feel any less like a monster.

She could feel the anger emanating from Shourya as he sat on the other end of the bed, looking away from her, his back stiff. She was already crying more than she had in years, but something inside of her needed a larger outlet. Tears were not making her feel any better. She wanted to tell him about her disease. She wanted to open up to him and tell him what she was going through. But just when she thought she could not keep it in any more, there was a knock on his door, and Shourya was called out for Shreela's bidaayi. He left the room without even turning to look at her.

Lavanya got up from the bed and went to the attached bathroom. The water that she splashed on her face was freezing and made her teeth clatter. She took her time with it though, washing away her make-up, letting the chill spread over her face till it was numb and the water ceased to feel cold. The towel she used to wipe her face smelled of Shourya.

He was right. She was selfish. She had always been. She had only thought of her own problems and tried to find a way to solve them. And running away was the only solution that had presented itself. After she had left the country, she had gone through hell. She had needed him desperately, and she knew he missed her too, but she did not want to be tied to her past any longer. She needed to move on. As did he. Lavanya had never thought she would return to India, and could not keep hurting him and herself by maintaining a friendship from thousands of miles away. She had cut him off intentionally, so he could have a life without her and the troubles she inevitably brought with her. He did not need all of her baggage bringing him down. She had stopped speaking to him so that he could move on.

And he had. He had found Deepti and he had been happy for a time; he had loved, and been loved back.

Maybe Shourya was right, maybe he should give Deepti another chance. Lavanya's intense protectiveness towards him should not stop him from having a real chance at happiness . . . with Deepti.

Lavanya wanted to cry. She was crying already, but she . . . wanted to cry. She wanted to let it all out, but she could not help but feel that no amount of tears would be able to quench the intense feeling of helplessness . . . and hopelessness within her.

A deadly disease was on its way to killing her. Shourya might be getting back with his ex. And judging by the things he'd said, he might not even want to talk to her again. This could quite easily be the worst time to realize she was in love.

Of course she loved Shourya. She had always loved him.

Lavanya felt suffocated. She wanted to get out of there. Like always, she wanted to run away from her problems. As she opened the bathroom door to get out, a T-shirt hanging behind it on a hook grazed her face. It was the blue one he had been wearing the day he had come to teach her how to play the guitar. She took it down from the hook, rolled it up and shoved it into her handbag.

There was a crowd gathered at the front gate to see off the bride, so she left through the back exit of the Kapoors' house. Lavanya had not said her goodbyes to Shreela and Manav, but that was the least of her concerns.

By the time she reached home, half an hour later, her feet had several cuts on them. She had tried to walk on the uneven roads for the first ten minutes, but it had proved impossible to run in five-inch pencil heels. She had given up and taken them off. People were staring at her, but at least it was still very early in the morning and there weren't many people on the road.

As soon as she opened the front door, Toughy jumped on her excitedly. Lavanya pulled him up to her chest and fell to her knees, weeping into his neck. Toughy whimpered softly and stayed in her arms instead of wriggling away. Lavanya felt an immense sense of thankfulness for the little dog; it had been years since she'd had a shoulder to cry on.

After a while, she stood up with him in her arms and went to her room. She did not want her parents to wake up and find her crying on the floor, clutching the dog. As she climbed the stairs quietly, she got very aware of her bangles jingling.

She found her father standing at the top of the stairs. He was wearing a full-sleeved T-shirt with his pyjamas. Lavanya did not look at him as she walked past him, hoping to avoid a scene.

'I thought I heard someone downstairs. Is the bidaayi over? Did everything go well?'

Lavanya was walking by him to her room, avoiding a confrontation, but when he spoke to her, she stopped to turn back and glare at him. *He was the reason why. He started all of this.*

His eyes were swollen and drowsy, but as she held his gaze, she saw them widen and become more alert. She was tempted to turn away, avoid looking into his direction as much as possible. She didn't. She had been rightly accused of running away from her problems. For once, she wanted to face it.

In a matter of seconds, the expression on her father's face changed completely. His eyes got wider and more aware, his lips parted. Maybe in disbelief, Lavanya mused. Disbelief that his own daughter was looking at him. Mr Suryavanshi took a step towards her. 'Lavi . . .? Are you okay? Have you been crying? Is everything all right?'

'No.' Lavanya grit her teeth.

'What is wrong?'

'Everything. Every-*freaking*-thing.' She spat out each word deliberately, venomously. 'Nothing is right here. And it is all because of you. *You* did this. You made me run away. You made me leave Mom alone, leave Shourya behind, deal with depression and loneliness and start doing . . . things I should not have done . . . It's been seven years! Yet here I am, still dealing with the consequences of *your* actions.'

Lavanya saw the horrified expression on her father's face. She did not wait for his response; she had already said more than she should have, more than she had intended to. She rushed to her room and shut the door, leaving her father and Toughy in the hallway. She flung herself on the bed face first and put a pillow over her head, trying to block out the world, and all that was wrong with it.

~

She had to get away. She had to run.

It had already happened. She knew it in her gut; something terrible had happened. Something she could not run from. Her legs betrayed her, they always did. She crawled to the door. She could not remember where she was, but it did not matter. If she could make it outside, she would find someone who could help her find her way back home.

She did not know where her wallet was and she still had not been able to locate her cell phone. Just as her fingers clutched the doorknob, she heard someone call her name. She turned around.

'Where are you going?' the man asked. He was standing with his back against another door. She had not noticed there was another door.

'What did you give me?'

'It's mind-blowing, isn't it? Blows your mind, like phew . . .' he gestured his mind being blown.

'What was it?' she asked, her voice cracking with desperation.

'Just coke. We snort mostly, but takes time. Smoking is faster. Shooting's even faster . . .' He pulled out a glass pipe from his pocket and waved it towards her.

'No, there was a needle . . .'

'Yeah, injecting is the fastest. Gets you off in like, three seconds.'

'I have never done that before.'

'Really?' He had already slumped down on the couch.

'Is coke bad?'

'Mmm?'

She leaned on the door. She could hear him snore within minutes. The fat guy on the floor had still not moved. Her eyelids kept drooping, she kept forcing them open.

She had to get up. She had to run.

Her hand slipped off the doorknob and she lost her balance, crashing to the floor. Her head hit the cold, hard ground.

The crash brought back some of her senses. She willed her arms to move, to support her as she got up. She begged her legs to not give up on her again. She had to get up. She somehow pushed herself back up. The motion drained her of all her energy, and the drug took over again.

This time she when her head hit the floor, she could not get up.

But somehow she knew . . . she had to run.

~

Shourya could not sleep for hours after Shreela left with Manav. He had already been distressed after his showdown with Lavanya. When Shreela hugged him and cried, he could not take it any more.

When had life become so complicated? Why did they have to be so far from the people they loved? Everything was changing. Now that Shreela's wedding was finally over, Shourya had to think about going back. He had only ten days left in Delhi before he had to return to California. He wondered what he would be going back to.

And what it would be like to come back home.

He had always planned to come back . . . he could easily find a good job in Delhi, or Bangalore or even Mumbai. Be closer to home, visit his family whenever he wanted. True, he still had a student loan to repay, which was easier and faster to do when he earned in dollars. If things went as planned, he would pay it back within two years and come back to India.

That had been *their* plan. He did not know what Deepti's plan was any more. She had been calling him all day. Shourya had been so focused on Shreela's wedding arrangements that he hadn't really thought about what Deepti had proposed. But now that the wedding was over, he had to make a choice. He wished he could talk it over with Lavanya. She had taken over all his actions and decisions regarding Deepti, but he'd driven her away.

When he had returned to his room, there was no trace of her there, except a faint hint of her perfume. He lay down on his bed, feeling dizzy. He should not have said all those horrible things to Lavanya and made her cry. As if she wasn't going through enough already. It was so tough to see her break down like that. He kicked himself for putting her through that.

When he fell asleep, it was a troubled sleep. He dreamt of Shreela in her beige lehenga and red dupatta, holding Manav's hand and walking away from him. He saw Lavanya running away from him again, leaving him at the airport without a second glance. And he saw Deepti snuggle into Avik's arms on the deck of a cruise, sailing away.

~

The insistent ringing of his phone woke Shourya up. He pulled out the wretched thing from under his pillow and picked up the call to make the shrill noise in his ears stop.

'Hello,' he muttered gruffly a moment later.

'Shourya, beta, is that you?' a female voice demanded from the other end.

'Mmm?'

'Hello? Shourya?'

'Hmm.' He managed to open his eyes. The room was dark and quiet. He was completely disoriented about where he was and what time it was. He pulled the phone away from his ear to see who the caller was. He did not recognize the number. He spoke into the phone, 'Yes, it's Shourya.'

'Shourya, this is Mrs Suryavanshi . . . Lavanya's mom.'

'Oh. Oh, hello Aunty. What is it? Is everything all right? Is Lavanya okay?' Shourya sat up on the bed. The only times he had received calls from Mrs Suryavanshi were when Lavanya was in some kind of trouble.

'Is Lavi with you?' Mrs Suryavanshi asked.

'No, she left here in the morning. Around five or six, I think.'

'Oh! We don't know where she could be,' her mother cried.

'What? Since when?' Shourya's heart beat loudly in his chest as he thought about the last conversation he had had with Lavanya. The hurtful things he had said.

'She left in the morning, around ten. She did not tell us where she was going, but she looked very upset . . . She hasn't taken any of my calls all day.'

Shourya checked the time on his phone. 6.23 p.m. Somehow despite all the craziness in his life, he had managed to exhaust himself and sleep all day. 'Don't worry, Aunty. I'm sure she's okay. It's not that late . . .' he said, getting out of bed.

'I'm worried about her, beta. She kept herself locked up in her room all morning. And then she left without a word.' Mrs Suryavanshi sounded distraught.

'She'll be back soon,' Shourya reassured her as he pulled on a shirt over his T-shirt. 'I'll—'

'I have never seen her this . . . troubled.'

'I'm going to look for her. And I'll talk to her.'

'She had a fight with her father this morning.' Mrs Suryavanshi's tone was timid and fearful.

Shourya froze.

'It was early in the morning. Soon after she came home from Shreela's bidaayi, I think. Neither of them told me what happened, but I heard them in the corridor. When I came out, she had already locked herself up in her room.'

Shourya gulped. If something happened to Lavanya . . . He could not think that way. He had to find her. If he let such thoughts come into his mind, they would paralyse him. 'I'm going to find her,' he said, more to him than to Mrs Suryavanshi.

'Toughy was whining at her door all morning, but she did not let him in.'

'I will find her. Please take care, Aunty, and don't worry about anything. I'll find her. I'm sure she's okay.'

As soon as he hung up, Shourya called Lavanya. There was no answer. He tried again, and was about to hang up when he saw lights blinking at the foot of his bed. Lavanya's phone lay on the floor. She must have forgotten it in his room in the morning. *'Darn it!'* he muttered under his breath. He quickly pulled on his jacket and grabbed his car keys. Where could she be? Delhi was so big; there were innumerable places where a person who wanted to get lost in the city could go.

Shourya could not think of a place to start from. As he got into the elevator, he tried to look for some clue to where she could be. Her phone was locked. The only place he could think of was their school, but he knew Lavanya had no love for it, so it would not make sense for her to go there. He could circle her street and the surrounding area, to see if she was taking a walk. But who took eight-hour-long walks? His palms were clammy and his forehead was beaded with sweat.

He ran to his car, and unlocked it. It made a sound, and he saw a startled Lavanya stand up on the driver's side of the car.

13

Lavanya's heart was pounding in her chest. She could not only feel it, she could also hear it. And it wasn't just because the sound from the car had alarmed her. It was because of the person standing in front of her.

She had not expected to see Shourya there. Although, now that she thought about it, it shouldn't have come as a surprise to find him in his parking spot at some point. The thought that he might come down and see her before she'd successfully gathered the courage to go up and face him had not crossed her mind once.

'What the—' Shourya muttered. He paused in his tracks for a second, before rushing to her. 'God! What are you doing out here in the dark? Do you know how worried everyone is about you?'

The words caught in Lavanya's throat. Shourya did not look angry any more. He looked concerned, ruffled, even frightened. *For her.*

He held her by her shoulders and studied her under the dim light coming from the street lamp outside the parking area. 'Are you okay?' he muttered.

She nodded rapidly, repeatedly.

'Oh God, Lavanya! Look at me. Lavanya, talk to me. Let me . . . I'm so sorry for saying all those things to you. I was . . . I was angry and frustrated . . . and it had nothing to do with you. I'm in a very bad place right now, and I needed an outlet, and you were there and I vented it out on you. I didn't mean any of it. I'm so sorry, I'm such an asshole—'

'Shourya . . . Shourya . . . *Shourya*!' Lavanya tried to make him stop, but he went on speaking, apologizing.

'No, no, listen to me! It was wrong of me to dump all that on you. As if you didn't have enough problems of your own. I feel like shit. Don't believe a word I said earlier, I was just being a jerk and blaming you for my problems . . .'

'SHOURYA!' Lavanya snapped, silencing him. 'Will you stop? You said nothing wrong. It doesn't matter why you said it or the way you said it. The fact is—you were right. I did all of those things to you. *I* was the asshole. And I deserved every word you said, it was a long time coming.'

'It's not like that . . .'

'No, you *are* right. I had my reasons, but should they have been enough for me to leave everything? I *was* selfish. I really was. You are right about me.'

'No, you're not. You were just a child. You were only looking for a way to be okay.' Shourya looked at her with such intensity in his eyes that she could not speak for a minute. Everything they had been through, everything she had shared with him, every moment they spent together—she could see it all in his eyes.

She remembered the time when, years ago, she had skipped her physical education class and left school early. She had found her father's car parked outside an unknown house. It wasn't until she saw the little board that said *Mrs & Mr Benoy Dey* on the gate that she realized it was her science teacher's house. She double checked the number on the car; it was definitely her father's. Lavanya wondered if Mrs Dey had asked her parents to meet her outside the campus. Science was not her strongest subject, but she had it under control. She did not understand the need of a parents–teacher meet.

Lavanya decided to wait for her parents to come out. As unusual as it was for a teacher to ask parents to meet off campus, it was very unlike her parents to do something school-related without telling her. For a minute, she had wondered if her father and Mrs Dey's husband worked together. That could explain Lavanya's dad being there. Or he could be in one of the other houses on the street and had not been able to find a better parking spot.

Lavanya kept thinking of scenarios. It was her nervousness about her performance in Mrs Dey's class that made her slide down the bonnet and walk towards the house. She was a bundle of nerves; her gut told her not to open the gate, to keep on walking all the way home. Whatever Mrs Dey had to say to her parents couldn't be that bad. She could go home and ask her dad where he had been, and what Mrs Dey had said.

She had taken seven steps—was it odd that she remembered even this tiny detail?—inside the gate, when she had noticed a movement on the first-floor window out of the corner of her eye.

When she remembered the moment now, she saw herself standing there, watching as realization struck her sixteen-year-old self. She saw herself look up to the source of the movement. And she saw her father looking down at her. She would never forget the expression on his face. He looked baffled for a moment, rooted to the spot, his hand on the drape. Then she saw him release a troubled breath and gasp for air. She saw his lips move and mutter her name. Lavanya didn't need to look away from his face to see that he wasn't wearing a shirt.

They had stood there, frozen, their eyes locked with each other. They must have been like that for only a few seconds, but Lavanya remembered it feeling like hours passed before her eyes, but she saw nothing, only her father's eyes. His horror-struck eyes filled with guilt, remorse, shock? She didn't know. And she never found out . . . She never looked into her father's eyes again. Until that morning.

Lavanya had run. As soon as they had broken eye contact, Lavanya had taken a step back, then another and another till her back hit the gate. Turning, she had fumbled with the latch on it and looked up one last time before she got out. 'Lavi, *wait*!' She knew her father was going to come after her. She saw him rush away from the window, and she had run.

'You were there,' she said to Shourya, angrily wiping away the stray tear that escaped down her cheek. 'When it happened. I came to you.'

'Don't think about it. Please,' Shourya whispered.

'You were on the cricket ground; I remember clearly. The PE class was going on. I ran back to you and interrupted your game. You were so mad at me.'

'Hey! I didn't know what was going on. And like you said, you interrupted my game.'

Lavanya looked up at Shourya. All the buttons of his jacket were undone. As were the top four buttons of his shirt; the rest were done wrong, leaving one hole empty at the bottom. He was wearing a deep grey T-shirt under it, which he had had for years. It was completely worn, torn at the edges and also had tiny holes on it at places. Lavanya wondered if he'd let her keep it.

That day, he had reluctantly left the cricket ground with her and she had dumped everything on him. Ever since then, everything that she had gone through, he had too. He had shared her confusion and her anger, and when news of the affair leaked, he had borne the bullying with her.

'I cannot believe what I did to you, after everything . . .' she said.

'Ah, it's all right. I'm a man. I got over it.' Shourya shrugged.

Lavanya knew he was pretending it was no big deal just so she would stop feeling so bad. 'No, Shourya, it was wrong. And I'm sorry I didn't see that before today.'

'Okay, enough. We're done discussing this now. It's all in the past, let's leave it there?'

Lavanya nodded.

Shourya finally let go of her shoulder, and she leaned into his chest. Her head was buzzing with snippets from their fight in the morning, and every moment since then and before that. It was exhausting. He wrapped his arms around her and held her tightly.

'Never do that again. Never disappear.'

Lavanya sniffed. She had cried enough for the day, and refused to let another tear slip out. She rubbed her cheek against his chest and felt the soft fabric of his threadbare T-shirt. She tried to nod, but he was holding her too tightly.

She felt his chuckle reverberate through his chest. 'Use words; nods aren't the answer to everything,' he said. She knew if she looked up, she would find him smiling.

'I won't disappear,' she promised. An image of her medical report flashed through her head. 'Without telling,' she added quickly.

'Not even after telling. And in case you're planning to shut me out again once you return to New York, tell me now,' Shourya pulled back and watched her expression.

Lavanya held his gaze for a second, as if contemplating, then pushed out her bottom lip and shrugged. 'Meh.'

Shourya pushed her away at once and made a show of being majorly hurt. Lavanya laughed, chasing him, trying to pull him back to her. He dodged her and got away. But he was laughing too.

'Before I forget, we need to call your mom and tell her you're alive. She's freaking out. Think of a story to tell her; I'm going to let you do the explaining.'

'Such a gentleman.' Lavanya watched Shourya as he dialled her mother's number.

~

'You cannot be serious.'

'Oh, but I am.'

'Lavanya, this is insane!'

'I know. That's the point.'

'No, no, no! This is *not* a good insane, this is a ridiculous insane!' Shourya studied the electric blue beast in front of him. 'Okay, let me get this straight. This is a 1000 CC motorbike. You bought it brand new from the store, paid in full, and . . . What are you going to do with it, exactly?'

They were in front of her house. Lavanya was on the other side of the bike, which stood in the middle of the narrow path that led to the main door, cutting the lawn in half. She ran her fingers over the windshield and looked at the bike gleefully. 'Always wanted to have one of these. Road trip? It's on my list. We could go to Rishikesh—I've heard they have lots of adventure sports stuff there. Or we could go to see the Taj Mahal? I've never been to Agra.'

'So basically, you want me to ride it and take you on a road trip?'

'Are you saying you have a problem with that?'

Shourya thought about it. 'It does sound like fun,' he relented.

'Then what are we waiting for? I checked everything. Rishikesh is about 223 kilometres away by road, and Agra is 212 kilometres away. But they are both in the opposite directions. So we can go to only one. In a day, that is. We could go to the other one on the next day.'

'Whoa. Slow down, there.'

'Yeah, yeah, I am not saying we *have* to, I am just saying we *could*. It all depends.'

'On?'

'What you want to do,' Lavanya said softly, looking at Shourya with large eyes.

'Don't make that face at me! Fine, we can go to Taj Mahal first, and see if going that far on a bike is worth the hassle.'

'Can we go to Rishikesh first? I've never been river rafting befo— Toughy, no!' Lavanya ran after her puppy, and pulled her slipper out from between his teeth.

'I have,' Shourya said absent-mindedly, checking out the bike in front of him. 'But I've not been to the Taj Mahal, which is a shame. It *is* one of the seven wonders.'

'Okay, fine. Tomorrow morning, first thing. It takes less than three hours to get there by road. We could get there in two!'

Shourya chuckled at Lavanya's enthusiasm. They had spent every waking moment in last couple of days hanging out with each other. Lavanya had insisted on carrying her to-do list everywhere, and she had checked off another item by shoplifting a lipstick from a mall. He found it strange that she should have such a thing on her list, but she said she had always wondered if the intimidating security systems in big malls actually worked.

She had expected the store security to arrest her and hand her over to the cops. Or at least for the buzzer to go off when they stepped out of the store, but nothing of the sort happened. Lavanya was visibly disappointed.

'Why not one hour? I could ride the bike at 200 kilometres per hour,' Shourya prodded.

'Are you serious? I don't think it's safe to drive over a hundred, is it?'

'We'll see.'

Shourya knew that even though she'd bought a superbike in a mad moment, and the idea of taking a road trip had her excited, she was going to freak out as soon as the speed touched eighty. He wasn't sure she even knew what a hundred felt like on a bike.

'Taj Mahal it is!' she said excitedly.

~

He was right. Only, it did not even take them to cross eighty for her to start panicking. Lavanya freaked out just hearing the sound of the engine.

Shourya reached her place at five in the morning as they had decided. As soon as he started the bike, the beast roared into life. The sound was loud enough to wake up the entire street. Shourya could feel the engine grow hot underneath, and he revved up the accelerator, making the engine growl even louder.

'Oh my God. What is happening?' Lavanya cried from the back seat.

'Just your bike starting up,' Shourya grinned.

'No. No, no, no. There is something wrong. It was not making this noise when the guy delivered it.'

'Did he ride it to your place?'

'I . . . don't know. But there is definitely something wrong with this. Do you think the silencer is broken?'

Shourya could tell by the tone and shrill quality of Lavanya's voice that she was terrified. He adjusted one of the rear-view mirrors so he could see her. It was dark outside, but the dull yellow light coming from the street lamps showed him Lavanya's petrified expression.

He brought her arms around his body and placed them on top of each other against the tank. 'Bend forward. You have to relax your back—you can't sit straight!'

'This feels so weird—'

'Hold on tight!'

'Wait, no!'

He couldn't hear anything she said after that. Her arms were clutching his stomach tightly in the beginning, but she relaxed gradually and held on to the tank instead. Shourya tried to let her ease into the experience, slowly increasing the speed as he felt her get more comfortable.

They did not stop even once on the way. Lavanya helped him with the directions by checking the GPS on her phone. With the roads empty that early in the morning, they reached Agra in a little over two hours.

The sky was lightening. They were on a road that gave them a nice view of the Taj Mahal. As Shourya pulled up and looked for space to park the bike, he asked, 'Do you see that?'

'What?' he saw Lavanya lift up her head from his back and look at him in the rear-view mirror.

'The sun.'

'Where?'

'East.' Shourya rolled his eyes. 'Trust you to ruin a perfect cinematic moment.'

'What? I wasn't looking,' Lavanya made a hurt face before she looked at the sun, which was starting to peek out of the clouds, lighting up the sky with an orange glow. Shourya parked the bike outside the accessible area; there was a sign stating no vehicles were permitted within 500 metres of the monument. Lavanya got down and stretched her arms.

After two hours of listening to the constant roar of the bike, they found themselves in sudden silence. Shourya's thighs and hands were warm from the heat of the vehicle, despite the December cold.

'That was . . . something,' Lavanya said.

'*This* is something,' Shourya pointed at the Taj Mahal.

The morning sun came out from behind the orange clouds and illuminated the city with a soft glow. The Taj Mahal stood before them, hiding under a translucent white veil of mist.

'Shall we?' Shourya asked.

Lavanya gave him her arm and they started walking towards the monument. He had seen innumerable pictures of it ever since he was a child, but it was only now, when he was so close to it that he realized the magnitude of it. If it could look this magnificent from half a kilometre away, he could only imagine what being inside was going to feel like.

The walk up to the entrance was lined with craftspeople selling souvenirs and all sorts of gift items, from small replicas of the Taj to necklaces, refrigerator magnets, embroidered handbags and handmade key chains.

Even though it was early morning, there were plenty of tourists around. Shourya was annoyed by the security checks and the long queue, but as soon as they were let inside, it was as if they had stepped into another era. The gardens were green and lush, the Mughal architecture exquisite. When they walked in through the east gate, the Taj Mahal stood before them in all its glory. Walking leisurely, almost in a daze, they took their time reaching the monument.

Still some distance from the Taj's entrance, Shourya paused, and held Lavanya's hand. 'Wait. Let's stay here?'

She didn't protest.

They moved to the side, and out of the way of the tourists. They were facing the sun, which had climbed up on the clouds and was shining brighter. It seemed almost lazy, the way it stood in the background, not harsh, not interfering with the cool breeze that made their hair dance. Hers shone with a red sheen, flying away from her face.

'So?' Shourya looked at her and asked. She had not spoken in a while.

'It's breathtaking, isn't it?' Lavanya gushed. She shivered and pulled her jacket closer to her body.

'You okay?' Shourya whispered.

She nodded.

'Again with the nod.'

'I'm okay. Much better than okay. I'm great,' Lavanya murmured, looking at him before turning her attention back to the clouds that seemed to change colour every few minutes.

It was as if the air cast a spell on the two of them. They did not care about seeing the Taj any more. They found a romance with the clouds and forgot everything else.

14

There was an overwhelming acidic smell in the room. She was finding it difficult to breathe. The smell was familiar in a way, but also very alien at the same time. Cat urine—that is what the room reeked of. But there was something else mixed with it, something sweet and sickening.

She stank of it too. Not only had she smoked it, she had also slammed it into her veins. She could feel it dance inside her, moving in her body, coursing in her blood. She had a strong impulse to slash her wrist and let the venom flow out.

She could feel the toxins in her body long after the effects of the coke had disappeared. Her hair, gathered in a chic bun at the nape of her neck the previous night, had come undone. It stuck to her face and neck. When she looked down her nose, she could see that her mascara had managed to reach the tip of it.

She supported herself on her knee, before clutching the doorknob and trying to pull her body up. Her legs refused to support her weight, but she did not give up. It took time, but eventually she managed to crawl her way outside. Once she reached the road, she ran.

She ran and ran and ran, but she could never run away from it. It was in her. It was a part of her, and it was there to stay.

~

Lavanya woke up with a jolt. Her hair was sticking to her skin, strewn all over her face, neck and chest. She pushed it away angrily and sat up. The nightmares needed to stop. She had forgotten the difference between memories and dreams. Were these nightmares just nightmares, or had the things she dreamt of actually happened? There was no way to tell. It's not like coke helps cognitive behaviour or memory.

She remembered how it happened. Diving into her studies, and then into work, she had only woken up to her need for a life and friends when she had been having a terrible time at the office. She knew most lawyers did cocaine to help them stay up and work, and they met up at the pub downtown every weekend to snort up. She thought that could be the opening she needed, and had forced herself a few times to go there. But she was never able to build up the courage to join her colleagues at the PSM table. That's when a man with a tiny ponytail had approached her. He worked at some firm on Wall Street; she had seen him around at the pub a few times. One night, after a particularly bad week at work, she had taken him up on his offer and joined him at a house party at his friend's place.

Her recollections of the party were mostly hazy. She remembered up till the part where she was snorting cocaine, she had done it a few times before in law school too. But she must have been very high to have agreed to inject it with a needle.

The dreams only served to distort her memories of that night further.

When Lavanya woke up the next morning, she found herself tired of running from everything, all the time. She decided she had had enough. She was prepared to face the realities of her life, and that meant she had to find courage to call up Dr Shah's office and set an appointment.

Lavanya had run away from AIIMS after getting the tests Dr Shah had recommended done. Ever since then, Dr Shah's secretary had been calling her daily to set an appointment with the doctor to read and understand the test reports and work on her treatment plan. But Lavanya had been ignoring her, fearing the reports. Those reports could be her death sentence. They were going to decide whether her disease could be controlled or if it had already proceeded to AIDS.

All reason told her that it could not have, not so soon. She did not feel particularly sick; her body ached, but it had to do with riding pillion in a crouched position on the long bike rides and the mixture of cold breeze and hot sun they had faced later that day.

If she was right about the time when she got infected, which she was sure she was, the disease had been diagnosed relatively early. Lavanya could not think of anything other than sharing a needle that could have infected her with HIV. She had had a quiet and dull life, except for periodic bouts of rebellion when she had lost herself in the sweet smoke of weed and the oblivion of white rum.

Lavanya picked up her phone and called the doctor's office before she chickened out again. As it turned out, Dr Shah's schedule was packed for the day, but her secretary managed to squeeze her in the next day. He also reminded Lavanya that her reports had been ready for a week. Lavanya promised him that she would pick them up from the hospital the same day.

Her next call was to Shourya, to see how the plan for the Rishikesh road trip was coming along. As soon as he picked up, she said, 'Next stop, Rishikesh!'

'Nope,' came the dreary response from the other end.

'Shourya.'

'Don't Shourya me. I'm not going. It's not going to happen.'

'Why can't we go? This is so unfair. You are no fun,' Lavanya complained.

'I'm okay with not being any fun as long as I don't have to ride that bike for 500 kilometres in a day,' Shourya said grumpily.

'You said we'd go to Agra first and see, and if it's worth it, then we'd go to Rishikesh. We had fun on the Taj Mahal trip, right? You said you did.'

'I did. But only up to the point when we got there and stayed outside. It was all downhill from there, and you know it.'

They had explored the monument and the Mughal architecture around it, but by the time they had finished, they had found themselves fighting to stay together. The place had got way too crowded for them to explore idly. After eating a breakfast that was incredibly greasy, but not delicious enough to make up for the excess oil, they had got back on the road. By the time they reached home, the sun had set. It had taken them twice as long on their way back because of the afternoon traffic. The sun added to the incredible amount of heat the bike generated and they had to take regular breaks to allow the vehicle to cool down and keep themselves from burning.

By the time they were back, their bodies were in knots. The weird position their spines had to stay in for hours did not help. Superbikes may be a lot of fun, but practicality is hardly their best quality.

'I get what you mean,' Lavanya relented.

Whenever she remembered that Shourya was be in Delhi for just one more week, she could not help but feel unnerved. She had not figured out what she was going to do yet. Whether she wanted to stay back here and get treatment, once the pretence of winter holidays was over, or return to New York and hide from her family again. Once Shourya left, she would have nothing to hide behind, and would either have to confront her parents or run away. She excelled in the latter, but was not sure if it was the answer, not this time.

She sighed. 'Still. We should do *something*. Or do you plan to waste the last one week you have here?'

'Don't worry. We will do something,' Shourya promised.

~

Sometimes, she was crippled with fear. Even though she spent most of her days actively trying not to think about AIDS, sometimes it became the only thing she thought about. And her days were getting more and more AIDS-y recently.

She had it. She *knew* she had it. She could feel it in her stomach the same way she could feel the venom moving through her veins the day she got infected with HIV. She did not have to open the envelopes she was holding to find out how bad it was.

Her hair was sticking to her scalp again. Lately, it had been sticking to any and every part of her body it could reach, at all times. She had never had a problem with sweating before, and she refused to let it pass as coincidental. *It was a symptom.*

Just like the whiteness of her palms. She had no blood in her body. AIDS was drinking all of it. When she pulled down her lower eyelid, all she saw was the palest pink. There was no sign of blood. Just like her skin, which was becoming a sickly shade of yellow.

She had the strongest feeling of having AIDS when she was at the hospital. On their first meeting, when Dr Shah had explained how HIV worked and how it caused AIDS, her stomach told her that the virus inside her had already caused AIDS. When she went back to the hospital to collect her reports, surrounded by sick people, she knew she was one of them.

It had started to show on the outside. The sweatiness, the paleness. It wouldn't be long before bigger symptoms started surfacing. She tried not to look at the other patients as she asked the receptionist if Dr Shah's schedule had an earlier opening and she could meet Lavanya sooner than appointed. There wasn't.

Lavanya intentionally walked past Dr Shah's office anyway, not sure what she was hoping to see. Through the tiny glass panel on the door, she could see the doctor speaking to two people sitting opposite her. Lavanya stayed there and watched Dr Shah gesture to explain something to her patients. How many times was Lavanya going to go to that cabin? How much time of her life would be spent there? Once they read the report and the level of her sickness was established, that was it. She would officially be an AIDS patient.

She gulped.

She could not run away from it.

~

Even before Shourya could knock on Lavanya's door, Toughy greeted him by hopping on him. He bent down to pick him up, but the puppy managed to wriggle out of his grasp and proceeded to limp around Shourya in circles. Shourya threw him off by running around him in circles instead, and the poor dog sat down, confused.

'What are you doing?' Lavanya asked. He found her standing against the half-open front door, head tilted questioningly.

'Don't judge! He started it.'

'I expect it from him; he's a dog. What's your excuse?'

'Loosen up!' Shourya picked up Toughy and was rewarded with a long lick on his cheek and a reasonable amount of tail wagging.

'He's being punished right now. He has been a bad dog, haven't you, Toughy?' Lavanya came to them and scratched

Toughy's ear. 'Aw, I can never stay mad at him. But he did poop on the carpet.'

'And you thought locking him out in the lawn would be a fitting punishment? Look at him, he's having a blast out here!'

'It's just who he is. I don't think he's capable of being sad.' She was looking lovingly at Toughy, a slow smile appearing on her lips. But it was she who looked sad. 'Give him to me.'

'Didn't you just say you were punishing him?' Shourya asked.

'Loosen up, dude,' Lavanya muttered and walked back inside.

Shourya couldn't see anyone else around in the house. Lavanya looked very subdued, and the fact that she had put Toughy out in the lawn and was alone at home made him suspicious. As he entered her room, Shourya asked, 'Is everything okay?'

'Yep,' Lavanya replied from where she sat on a little plush sofa in the corner with Toughy.

'Aunty, Uncle—everybody?'

'Yep,' she repeated, not meeting his eyes.

Shourya fought the urge to ask her what she was doing, coming out of AIIMS that morning. He had a feeling that something was wrong with either her mother or father. Her refusal to look at him, and keeping things from him annoyed him.

'What did you do all day?' he asked, studying her closely.

'The day has just started,' she said and looked up at him. 'What is the plan? Are we going to do something fun today, or just waste away the rest of your time here?'

'We could stay in and watch something. Maybe take it easy for a day or two?'

'If that's what you want. How come you've become so dull lately? You sound like me nowadays. Always saying no to fun, exciting stuff and choosing to hang out and do boring shit.'

'You are underestimating the power of doing lazy things. Have you seen *Troy*?' Shourya asked.

'You mean the city in New York? Haven't been there.'

'Lavanya Suryavanshi!'

'What?' she asked, looking at Shourya's bewildered expression. 'What is it? Why are you looking at me like that? What did I say?'

'Are you telling me,' Shourya said slowly, deliberately, 'that you have not heard of *Troy*? The movie? One of the highest grossers at the box office? Brad Pitt as Achilles? Rings a bell?'

'I think I must have heard of it somewhere around, but—'

'You *think* you . . . No. No, absolutely not! Lavanya, this is unacceptable. You have to watch it. I cannot believe you have not seen it already. We'll still be friends after this, but you need to rectify your mistake right now.'

'God! What's with all the drama!' Lavanya got off the sofa and placed Toughy back on it. The puppy had dozed off, and Lavanya patted his neck once before walking to the TV and turning it on.

'Dude! You're taking this too lightly. It's not like *Troy* is a masterpiece or anything, but it is for me. For most people actually, it is fairly average. But take my word for it, it is everything you look for in a movie. Everything you can ask for.'

'Fine, let's watch it. Do you know anywhere we can buy it online? Amazon?'

'So much enthusiasm,' Shourya said, but immediately started looking for the movie online. He knew she would understand once she watched it.

'Don't feel bad; it's not this movie. It's all of them. I don't remember when the last time I saw a film was,' Lavanya said. Then added, 'Could have been here, with you.'

'Seriously? You haven't seen a single movie since school? Are you . . . never mind.'

'Am I, what? Say it.'

'Nothing. I was thinking you cannot be serious. But having got to know you again, I think you are capable of being that person,' Shourya said. Back in school, they used to watch movies every weekend. When they did not have any pocket money left to go to cinema halls, they would wait for the movies to be leaked on illegal torrent sites and then download and watch them at home. Having movie marathons was their weekly ritual.

'I have not changed that much. I just did not have time for all this.' Lavanya was speaking mostly to herself.

'Be that as it may. I'm putting *Troy* in your to-do list, and we're going to tick it off right now.'

They bought *Troy* online and started watching it together. Mrs Suryavanshi came home after some time and was happy to provide them refreshments. Shourya watched Lavanya closely during the movie. As they entered the second hour, he noticed her become more and more involved in it. He thought the best way to start watching a movie was to begin with low expectations and then let it blow your mind. Although he had recommended it to her very highly, she had not seemed very impressed. In fact, Shourya had the feeling that she had agreed to watch it only because he asked her to, and she had nothing better planned. She had not seemed enthusiastic at all.

He had bought the extended version, and once they were halfway through it, she refused to pause it even to let him take a phone call. By the time they reached the legendary Hector versus Achilles duel scene, Lavanya was sitting up on the bed and her eyes were glued to the screen. She kept muttering *no, no, no*.

When they reached the part where Achilles and Briseis get intimate and Brad Pitt delivers full back nudity, Shourya was surprised that Lavanya did not show even the slightest discomfort watching it with him. In fact, she was so involved, he wasn't sure she even realized that he was in the room with her.

When the movie ended and the slow music played as credits rolled, Lavanya slumped back on the bed and sighed.

'So?' Shourya asked, even though he did not really need to—his answer was all over her face. 'What did you think?'

'Whoa!' she said, staring at the ceiling with wide eyes.

'I know, right? It is so underrated. It's like the most underrated action movie of all time. But there's just something about it. It's a package. The perfect amount of action, romance, mythology, drama, thriller—everything. And gore. I need my movies gory.'

'*Troy* wasn't a super hit?'

'It was, I guess. But it didn't receive a lot of critical appreciation. They thought it was too glamourized and superficial or something.'

'That's insane. There was depth. The whole Hector–Achilles chemistry, and Briseis . . . that was deep, for sure,' Lavanya said.

Shourya could see her replaying it in her head. 'Let me guess. Achilles was your favourite character, right?'

'Nope. Hector's my favourite.'

'You're just saying that because you don't want to sound shallow by admitting that you fell for Brad Pitt's good looks.'

'Shut up!' Lavanya sat up again. 'I love Brad Pitt, of course—doesn't everybody? And I loved Achilles because he reminded me of Salman Khan. But honestly, Hector was the only one in there with something in his head. He knew what was going to happen, right from the beginning, but no one listened to him. Not that loser Paris, or his own father, the king, whatever his name was. If they had just listened to what Hector was saying the entire time . . .'

Lavanya sat there, shaking her head, as if deep in thought. Shourya smiled at her enthusiasm. He had missed being with her, having her around all the time. Then, much like now, they would spend all day together and not tire of each other's company, even if they did nothing exciting.

'I have five more days before my flight back . . . We can take a trip somewhere if you want, as long as I do not have to drive in the heat.'

Lavanya's spun around to face him. 'Really? Like we can take a flight somewhere?'

'I was thinking, more like go nearby with a tour company or something. Or drive down somewhere, but . . .'

'Oh, Shourya, what happened to your sense of adventure?' Lavanya stuck out her lower lip.

'What is so adventurous about travelling in an airplane?'

'It's the destination that's exciting. We can go to Goa! It's the best time for it too. Spending New Year's Eve there— it would be perfect. There are music festivals and so many beaches. It could be really fun.'

'I've been to Goa before. There's really not much to see a second time,' Shourya said. Living in the Bay Area, he had developed a fascination for beaches, but from what he remembered of his trip to Goa with his family back when he was fourteen or fifteen, he had not had even the least bit of fun. His entire extended family was there, and they had spent most of their time arguing about what sites to visit and where to eat.

'Fine. You stay here. I'm going to go alone,' Lavanya said.

'You're not going alone!'

'Why not?'

'Because it's not safe.'

Lavanya snorted. 'Like anything is. I am not going there to be *safe*. I am going there to have fun. And if you won't come with me, I'll go by myself.'

'Why is it always the extremes with you?' Shourya asked in exasperation. 'Fine, I'll come with you.'

'I *knew* it.'

'Yeah, manipulation *is* becoming your strong suit.' Shourya rolled his eyes. 'It isn't a good colour on you though, just so you know.'

'You're just easy to manipulate,' Lavanya responded, winking at him. 'And I want to make the most of your time here. Who knows when we will get such a chance again?'

When Shourya looked at her, he wanted to say something, to respond to her hypothetical question, but he didn't know what to say. The way she talked about them having fewer opportunities to spend time with each other in the future made him wary. It felt like she was abandoning him again, and he was stuck there trying to say something, to explain to her . . . something that he himself did not understand.

15

Lavanya looked up at the apartment one more time. It was a colour that must have been white at one time, but had faded, become dirty and developed a mud-like quality to it. The balcony they were ogling was covered entirely with what looked like a thick brown canvas that hid everything from view. The word *Roxan* was painted in red, cursive letters underneath. She wondered what it meant. They had been there since morning, waiting for a glimpse.

When she had first told Shourya that she had booked a flight to Goa via Mumbai, she hadn't told him that there was a twelve-hour halt in Mumbai. They took an early morning flight to Mumbai and it was only when they landed there that Lavanya told him the truth. It was only 8.30 a.m. and their flight to Goa was at 9.15 p.m. Shourya was not amused.

He asked her how she could not notice the difference in time between connecting flights before booking the tickets and she tried to fool him by saying she thought it said 9.15 a.m. He realized what it was really about when she suggested that since they were there and had a whole day, they should stake out Salman Khan's apartment in Bandra.

It was not easy to convince him, but Lavanya played her I'll-go-alone card one more time. Lavanya thought he caved in because he didn't see what good hanging back at the airport or roaming around Mumbai alone would achieve anyway. His only condition was that they had to have vada-pav before they did anything else.

Lavanya's stomach, which was always ready for food, did not seem to agree that morning. She could barely make it through one of them before her palms started sweating. She *knew* it was a symptom of her disease, but tried to suppress the thought. She had the rest of her life to worry about dying, but only five more days with Shourya. She could agonize about AIDS when they got back home.

'Listen, Lavanya, I don't know what kind of kick you're getting out of this, but it's hot out here. We have been roasting for the last six hours. Don't you think we should just check out the beach, or Marine Drive or something and go back to the airport?' Shourya asked. He was looking at her with pleading eyes. She could see the skin on his cheeks had turned red. They had discarded their sweaters and jackets as soon as they got out of the airport. The city of Mumbai was unfamiliar with the concept of winter.

'We have to stay. He's in there, I know it. You know my gut is never wrong,' she said.

'What about the time you thought India was going to win the cricket World Cup in 2003? We lost *so* badly. So badly, it's not even funny.'

'We made it into the finals and we were going to win, it was written in the stars. It's just that none of the players performed. None. Not one. How did they expect to win without playing?'

'That's not the point. The point is—your gut isn't as trustworthy as you think it is. And I don't want to waste another four hours outside this sad little apartment waiting to see an actor I don't even like,' Shourya declared.

'Okay, wait.' Lavanya had to take a minute to collect her thoughts before speaking. 'So many things wrong with what you said. First, my gut is almost always right. Second, we are not wasting time, we are bonding—this is precious time that will not come back. Third, this apartment is not sad; it must cost crores and crores of rupees. Fourth, it is hardly little. Fifth, you can't *not* like Salman. You don't get the liberty to decide that.'

Shourya glared at her. 'Don't care. I'm leaving. You can come if you want, otherwise I'll see you at the airport, or in the airplane, depending on the amount of time you choose to waste in this wretched place.'

'Again with the hating! You could have just said this place. Why call it bad names?' When she received more glares in response, she switched tracks. 'You're not actually going to leave me here alone, are you?'

'If you make me, yes.'

'You won't.'

'Are you coming or not?' Lavanya gauged Shourya's expression. He looked pretty darn serious. Maybe she had pushed him too far this time. She weighed her options. She wanted to see Salman Khan desperately, but staying there did not guarantee that. And even if he was inside, which her instinct told her he was, there was no certainty that he was coming out any time soon.

On the other hand, if Shourya went away, she would be left alone with her thoughts, which, frankly, had been nothing but depressing recently. Also, despite his mood, which had been irritable since arriving in Mumbai, she had been enjoying spending time with him and did not want him to go. She bit her lower lip. She was going to have to yield.

'Fine,' she muttered. 'If you are going to be a bully, there is nothing much I can do about it. Have it your way.'

'My way?' Shourya looked at her incredulously. 'Trust me, of all the ways in the world, camping out in front of some brash celebrity's apartment building is the last thing I would have done had I actually got to do things my way. This is my attempt to salvage whatever's left of the day.'

'You are being so impossibly rude right now, I don't even want to look at you. I mean, seriously, it was just a few hours out . . . in the . . . What is happening?' Lavanya got distracted by the sudden rush of fans towards the building.

The crowd gathered outside Salman's apartment building had been growing larger all day. Some of them had started running towards the gate and the others looked confused about what was happening, just like Lavanya. It was a little after five in the evening and the sun was riding low. Lavanya looked at the balcony they had been observing all day and found the canvas enclosure still shut.

Shourya held her hand and crossed the road. They could tell by the excited exclamations around that someone was coming out. Lavanya's heart raced as she held Shourya's hand and stood on tiptoes to get a look.

There was a white Range Rover coming out of the building's parking lot. She had memorized the registration number of Salman's car and . . . *This was it!* More and more people were joining them and she was getting squished, but she did not care. She had dreamt of this moment all her life. She was going to see the one man in the world who could make her want to fall in love.

The first time she had seen *Maine Pyar Kiya* was the first time she had thought about love. She was a teenager, and the movie was relatively old—released two years before she was born—29 December 1989. She could not believe she was there twenty-five years later, on the anniversary of *Maine Pyar Kiya*'s release, seeing Salman Khan in front of her!

All she saw was his back. He was wearing a black short-sleeved T-shirt with a pair of blue jeans and black high-top sneakers. She could see the veins of his arms bulging, and his T-shirt was stretched over the muscles on his back. Lavanya felt faint. She only saw him for about three seconds before he disappeared into the car. But that was enough.

In a few seconds, the car disappeared out of sight completely. The crowd collected there began to scatter and some policemen tried to restore balance to the havoc they had caused on traffic.

Lavanya fell back. Shourya pulled her away from there. Out of everything she had done to tick off points in her list, this one had proven to be the most fulfilling. It was her childhood dream come true!

~

Shourya chose not to say it. It was tough, but Lavanya looked so ecstatic to have seen her only hero in person, that he did not want to ruin if for her. He wasn't sure about it anyway, so there was no reason to put doubt in her head.

When 'Salman' had stepped out of the Range Rover for a few seconds to wave at the crowd, he had his back to where they had been standing, and they could not see his face. Shourya had strong suspicions that the man could have been either of Salman's brothers—Arbaaz or Sohail. They did look wider than he would expect Salman to be, but celebrities always tend to look different on screen than in real lives. There was confusion in the crowd too, but give Indians any celebrity, no matter how big or small, they go crazy. He hailed a taxi to take them to Juhu beach, which was relatively close to the airport.

'I told you he was in there! My gut is always right. You should always trust me,' Lavanya said, her first words since they left the area in front of Salman Khan's apartment half an hour ago.

Shourya looked at her in the darkness of the cab. She was literally glowing, her cheeks were flushed and her ears red. 'Lesson learned,' he said.

They spent the rest of their journey to the beach in silence. Once there, she took her shoes off and they decided to walk along the sea. It turned out that walking barefoot on the beach was a big mistake; tar balls from ships and the waste tourists created was scattered across the portion of the beach they were strolling on. But Lavanya refused to put them back on. She said that having wet sand beneath her feet and leaving footprint trails was one of her favourite things in the world.

They watched the sun set and then took a cab back to the airport. Although they weren't saying much, Shourya was really enjoying her silent company. He could feel the air change between them. It wasn't how it used to be when they were in school, or how it had been when they met again three weeks ago. It was something he had not experienced before. It confused him, in an exciting kind of way.

When she rested her head against his shoulder as they waited for their flight at the gate, and then again on the plane, it felt like the most natural thing in the world for her to do. Together they sat, Shourya in the middle seat and she at the window, her head resting on his shoulder, and they observed the dark clouds outside, which seemed to be running away from them.

'What are you going to do?' she whispered, her eyes closed.

'About what?' he asked.

'Deepti and Avik.'

Ever since Shreela's wedding, when they had their huge fight, he hadn't brought up Deepti with Lavanya or called

her. In fact, for the first time in months, he hadn't thought
of her at all, not even in passing. He remembered how, no
matter where he was and what he was doing, he used to think
of her all the freaking time—that wasn't happening to him
any more.

'Do you know what I think?' Lavanya murmured.

Shourya looked down at her. The highlights in her hair
appeared a dull red under the dimmed lights, looking almost
black. Her eyes were still closed and her lips moved softly as she
spoke. Her bare face, stripped of make-up, looked as innocent
and vulnerable as a child's. She looked like the seventeen-
year-old girl he had fallen in love with all those years ago—the
thought came to his mind unbidden.

'Not really,' he said.

'I think you still live with them because you cannot deal
with her not being in your life any more. You need her to be a
part of your life, in any way possible, so you live with them in
the same apartment, even though it means dealing with their
bullshit regularly.'

She continued, 'And also because you want them to
remember you. No . . . you want *her* to remember you. You
want to keep being a part of her life, and occupy her mind.
You want her to feel pain because she made you feel pain.
You think the guilt of what she did to you will bring her back
to you one day.'

Shourya had no words. He had never thought of such an
explanation to his behaviour. He did not think that she was
right about everything, but he could not entirely dismiss what
she was saying either. There was truth there. He just didn't
know how much.

Maybe prompted by his silence, Lavanya removed her
head from his shoulder and studied his face. She reached for
his hands and held both of them with one of hers. She sighed

before saying, 'You're going back to her, aren't you? If you haven't already.'

'Nothing of that sort. In fact, I haven't decided what I'm going to do about her. I've not been thinking too much—'

'Look, it's okay. I get it. I don't know anything about her, nothing more than what you've told me, anyway. But from what I know, you are very much in love with her. She's your one true love . . . meant for each other and all that. I just want you to be careful. I want you to be happy, and if being with her makes you happy, that is what you should do. I can tell by the way you still defend her, after everything, that you will never stop caring for her, so why fight it?'

It hurt Shourya. It physically hurt him, the way she said it so casually. Lavanya had no idea how he felt about her, and here she was . . . telling him to go back to Deepti, who felt like a distant memory now. He could not believe how messed up he had been because of her just a month ago, and how hollow he had felt. But that void was no longer there. He had found the one he truly wanted, had always wanted, the one that got away . . . He'd got a second chance—

'Go back to her. Don't waste time, you've already lost so much of it because of all the drama with Avik and all that. Put an end to it.'

'I fired you, remember? You no longer get to make my decisions for me.'

She did not say anything else for the rest of the flight. They landed after some time and as soon as they reached their hotel, they said goodnight in the living area of their suite and went to their separate rooms. Shourya was grateful for the heat he had roasted himself in the whole day and the resulting exhaustion—it made him fall asleep as soon as he got into bed.

16

Lavanya could not sleep that night. After the Salman Khan incident, her excitement had slowly faded away. The evening had turned into a very calm and lazy affair. Spending time with Shourya without having to talk, walking along the beach in silence had been wonderful—the only thought that scared her was the thought of him going away in a few days.

In that moment, she realized just how much she loved him. He was strong, caring and sensitive. Whenever he was around her, he automatically took care of her and watched her back. She felt safe with him. He was someone she could depend on, more than herself. Someone she had blind faith in. Someone who would never break her heart, the way she'd broken his so many years ago. But the fact was that whether he chose to take Deepti back or not, and whether she was in New Delhi or New York, he would be thousands of miles away, in California. Having him back, depending on him once again, had felt so good, and now it was almost at an end.

In her panic of losing him, she had tried to ask him about his plans, and had somehow ended up asking him to go back to Deepti. She wondered all night what that was about, and came to the conclusion that she was letting him go before he went away anyway. She did not know if Shourya would ever again feel what he had once felt for her. Even if by some miracle he did, she did not have a chance at a normal life and it wouldn't be fair to him to involve him in her problems.

Lying in her bed, she contemplated going to his room and talking to him. They had taken up a suite with two bedrooms separated by a bathroom. For a minute, she even thought of telling him about her disease. That would probably make him stay, at least for a little while longer. He would pity her and give her a few more days of his company. She wasn't going to deny she wanted that.

She padded to his room and pushed the door open, only to find him fast asleep on the bed. She walked in and sat next to him for some time. She could barely see him in the darkness, but enough to feel a sharp pain in her chest. How would she live without him, again? The first time had almost killed her; she was not sure she could survive being away from him again.

In that dark moment, she resolved to tell him about her medical condition. But once she did that, she could not tell him that she loved him, because that would put him in the impossible position of choosing between staying with a dying person or abandoning her.

Lavanya wanted to touch his face. She wasn't sure if she would get a chance to do that ever again. But she stopped herself. She had come to realize that there were a lot of things in the world she could not have, and she had no choice but to make peace with that. She got up from the bed and walked away, without looking at him. The longer she stayed, the more hurt she would be. Back in her room, she sank down to the floor at the foot of the bed in a crumpled heap. She could feel herself breaking—her willpower to fight, her desire to live, her heart.

～

Lavanya heard a knock at her door. She slipped soundlessly from under the sheets and reached for a wet wipe to clean her face. She could not risk going to the bathroom they were sharing. After a night spent crying on the floor, she had barely slept for two hours before waking up again, preparing herself mentally to come clean to Shourya. Her face looked warped— eyes and lips swollen, dark shadows under her eyes—and she suspected her migraine was somehow visible too.

She was creeping back under the comforter when Shourya knocked a second time. She leaned back against the head rest and said, 'Yes, come.'

'Good morning!' Shourya greeted cheerfully as he entered, a grin on his face. He was wearing a white T-shirt with UC Berkeley printed across the front in black, bold letters.

Lavanya had a sudden vision of him preparing a breakfast tray for her while she slept peacefully—in a parallel world where they were in love and she wasn't sick. But he was not carrying breakfast with him that morning. The thought made her want to hide her face under the comforter and cry. 'Morning,' she said.

'What's with you?' Shourya asked. She saw the expression on his face change from concern to alarm as he looked at her. 'Are you okay?'

She had been foolish to think a face wipe was going to rid her of all signs of distress. This was Shourya. He could figure out she was sad from even the slightest downward curve of her lips. Lavanya was surprised that she had been able to keep something as enormous as this hidden from him in the first place. It had been easier when they hadn't been sharing a hotel suite. Now she had nowhere to run.

Nor did she want to.

Shourya sat down on the bed, facing her. It took all of her willpower to stop herself from reaching out and touching his face.

'What is it?' he asked.

She could not say it. She could not say anything. She could not tear her gaze away from his.

'Tell me. Lavanya, talk to me.' His voice was gruff, and there was desperation in it.

They had something in common then. She felt the same sense of anxiety inside her too.

She sniffed. Her lower lip started to quiver.

Shourya held her by her shoulders, the same way he had that night in the parking lot. Lavanya broke eye contact. She could not bear to look at him, knowing he wouldn't be a part of her life . . . She looked down at her lap, and lifted her hand to her throbbing temple.

Shourya pushed it away. He held her chin and tilted it upwards. 'Speak.'

Lavanya saw him grind his jaw. She was confused; she didn't know whether he was angry or annoyed or concerned. 'I can't . . .' her eyes pleaded with his.

'Yes, you can. Be honest with me for once! I know something is going on in that head of yours. What is it?' he demanded, clearly angry with her, but she couldn't fathom why.

She collected herself and began to speak. 'Shourya, I cannot do this to you. You . . . you have a life, and you are going back to it in four days. I cannot expect you to disrupt your life for me. You have to leave . . . you have to go back to Deepti.'

'You don't get to decide that,' he responded, pulling his hands away from her.

'But you will. It is the decision that you will make.'

'How do you know that? Just because *you* want me to go, you're telling me to get back together with her. I never said that was what I wanted.'

'But you love her. You told me you do.'

'That was before.'

'Before what?'

Shourya was not looking at her. This time Lavanya put her hand under his chin and turned his face towards her, the same way he had done to her many times.

'Before what?' she repeated.

'Don't make me say it, damn it! I tried to say it once and you asked me not to. Now I'm asking you not to force me to,' Shourya huffed. He ran his fingers through his hair and looked up at the ceiling. His nostrils were flaring with every breath he took.

Lavanya could not look away from him; it was as if she had lost all control of herself. Her hand dropped from his chin when she realized what he had just said. Her heart stopped beating for a moment. And started beating again at twice the pace. 'Shourya?' she murmured.

'If you can't see it yourself, if you're *that* blind, I don't think my explaining it to you will do any good.'

Every moment Lavanya had spent with Shourya flashed in front of her eyes. From the time they first met, till the time he had come to the airport to see her off when she was leaving for Harvard. He was crying unabashedly. He had managed to get an airport pass for the night, so once Lavanya said her goodbyes to her parents, he came with her all the way to the departure gates. After they collected her boarding pass and checked in her luggage, they got a cup of instant noodles from one of the stalls and sat down in a relatively isolated corner. She refused to meet his eyes. Her own filled with tears over and over again, but she did not let a single drop flow out. She kept blinking to hold them back. He concentrated on the cup of noodles they were sharing and she did the same. They pretended to be okay, and they succeeded . . . just as long as they didn't have to look at each other.

But then their time was up. Her flight was called to board. She looked down at her watch, and without a word to each other, they got up. That's when she had seen Shourya's eyes. They were red and haunted. His lips were tightly sealed into a thin sad line. Lavanya had never seen him that miserable before. He had always been the strong one. That was the moment she realized the extent of what she was doing to him. That was the first time she had wondered if she was making a huge mistake.

Shourya had been asking her not to go for months. She had begged and pleaded with him to stop saying that because her decision was final and as her friend, he should have been happy for her and supported her. And that's what he had done, minus the few bouts of weakness when he would ask her if this was what she really wanted, if she had thought it through and if there was no other way. She had known he did not want her to go, but she had thought it was mostly because he was worried about her. But that night at the airport, when he pulled her into his arms and rested his head on hers, leaning on her as if unable to support his own weight, that was when she realized just how much she was hurting him. But it was too late. She could not imagine returning home, to her old life.

She had felt his body heave as he held her that night. Felt his heart race and his breath come in gasps. When she tried to pull out of his embrace, he did not let her. He had kept on holding her. She had seen him break, right in front of her, in her arms. When he finally let her go and she looked up at him, she could tell from his pained expression that he was trying very hard to keep it together. He looked like a little boy, the kid she had met in kindergarten. The kid she had known all her life.

She could not look at him after that. He had walked with her till the queue at immigration. They stood there like a pair of statues, unresponsive, looking straight ahead. But he held her hand. When she was called, she gave him a half hug, stole her hand out of his and walked forward without looking at him.

She had felt his presence, but she was not strong enough to turn back. After she was done at the immigration counter, she moved ahead, and kept walking until she was sure he would have lost track of her in the crowd. She knew he would not leave as long as he could see her, and she would not have been able to board her flight if he was still at the airport. She hid behind a wide pillar and searched for Shourya, and when she spotted him in the crowd, standing exactly where she had left him, she saw he was looking for her too. She fought the urge to run back to him and put him out of his misery. He had searched for her for five more minutes before his head drooped to his chest, before walking away.

Thinking about that night now, she could not hold back her tears any longer. The image of him walking away, as he had so many times before—but always returning the next day—tore at her heart. That time, she was going too far away, somewhere he would not be able to reach her whenever he wanted, or she needed. That was when she had realized that she had to break ties with him. Despite what Shourya seemed to believe, she had not planned on it all along.

When she had left then, she had thought that the pain they were feeling was only momentary, and they would be okay in a few weeks. She had realized how badly mistaken she was only when she got him back. And now she could not let him go again.

'I love you too,' she said, before she could stop herself.

Shourya's head shot up, his eyes narrowed questioningly, as if searching for answers in hers.

'Yes, I do. I love you. I have run away from it for too long, and there are so many reasons we cannot be together, but I am tired now. I am so tired of running from you. I love you. I always have . . . I just didn't know.'

~

Shourya could not believe what he was hearing. Lavanya loved him. She loved him. After all this time. No matter how many times he repeated it in his head, he could not make sense of what was happening.

They had met by chance, on trips to their hometown that coincided, otherwise would they even have got in touch again? He doubted it. But ever since she had come back into his life, everything had changed. She had changed it. She had changed *him*.

When he had come home, he had been hurt and confused, even morose. But as soon as he had met her, his days had got better, his nights easier. They did not waste any time falling back into their old pattern, and before he knew it, his feelings for her had come rushing back. He could not have her in his life and not be in love with her. He did not know how to do that.

'Aren't you going to say something?' she asked. Her eyes were wide and sad, like a scared puppy's. It was as if she was expecting him to . . . hurt her?

'Do you mean it?' he asked.

Lavanya nodded.

Shourya couldn't wait any longer; he couldn't handle any distance between them, not even the mere inches that separated them right then. He pulled her close to him and wrapped his arms around her tightly. She melted into his arms and broke down. He held on to her tightly and muttered, 'I love you. I love you so much.'

Lavanya dug her head deeper into his chest and sobbed.

'No. No, no, no. Don't cry. It's okay. It's all going to be okay,' he whispered in her ear.

She shook her head vehemently, her hair tickling his nose.

'You've got to stop doing that, dude,' he tried to lighten up the mood.

'Can't,' came the muffled response. Her head kept shaking.

'Why not?'

'Your T-shirt feels nice against my forehead.'

Shourya chuckled.

When Lavanya pulled away and looked at him, he saw her smile at him, although reluctantly. He wiped her cheek and murmured. 'You've been crying too much.'

Shourya had never seen such an odd expression on her face. She came closer to him, close enough for them to feel their breaths on each other's face. Her lips parted. She touched her nose with his, before closing her eyes. Shourya's lips parted too. He moved closer to her on the bed and eliminated the little space that remained between them, pressing his lips to hers. Shourya moved his lips on hers, sucking her lower lip. She responded with a moan.

He was able to appreciate the meaning of the phrase *time paused*. He was in the moment, completely lost in her. She was the only thing he saw, even with his eyes closed. He sat up on his knees, pulling her with him. They were facing each other, their heads resting against each other's, their noses touching, and their breaths mingling, their knees sinking into the plush mattress. She arched her back, and he leaned into her, making her belly nestle softly against his stomach.

Shourya's hands slid up her back and he wrapped his hand in her hair, slowly caressing the nape of her neck. Her skin felt delicate and hot under his fingertips. He saw goosebumps rise on her arms as he traced circles on the skin at the back of her neck with his fingers. Her mouth parted, gasping for air. He teased her like that for a while, enjoying the power he held over her. He tugged on her hair, causing her head to fall back, bent over her and kissed her eyes, which closed at the touch of his lips. Her ragged breathing that matched his own gave him immense satisfaction.

Her hands, which had been on his neck, moved downwards, grazing his collarbone before resting on his chest. He could feel his heart beat beneath her hand, quickening every second. He released her hair and moved his fingers to her cheeks, grazing her lips with his thumb and then pulling her bottom lip down. She sucked at his thumb.

That was the last straw. He was done being gentle. He slid his hand down to her waist and pulled her flush against him; their bodies touching from shoulder to knee. His other hand tilted her face up to meet his mouth and his lips descended on hers hungrily, tasting her on his tongue.

She was panting. She tried to free herself from his embrace, but he did not let her move even an inch away from him. His mouth assaulted hers, his tongue pushing against the resistance her teeth put up. He could tell exactly how it was affecting her from the way her body moved against his—rising up to meet him and then pulling back.

'Shourya . . .' she managed to exclaim when he let her come up for air. 'Too much . . . too fast . . .'

'I know,' he whispered into her ear, before nipping it with his teeth.

'Ahh,' Lavanya yelped.

Shourya licked where he had bitten, to soothe the sting. She shivered against him, her breasts heaving against his chest as she held on to him. Shourya left a trail of kisses along her jaw, before returning to her lips. She tasted sweet and salty and amazing. Like winter air. He could not get enough. No matter how much she pleaded with him to go slow, no matter how hard he tried, he could not hold back. She was meant for passion, not tenderness.

He clutched her T-shirt in both hands, and whipped it off in one swift motion. He saw the surprise in her eyes, but she didn't protest. This was Lavanya—the girl he had been in love with for as long as he could remember, even though he'd only realized it much later. He was now holding her in his arms. The thought sent chills up his spine. He did not know what secrets she was keeping, or what tomorrow would bring. But in that moment, she was in his arms and she was in love with him. He had never felt so happy, yet so scared at the same time.

She was beautiful. Her skin was soft and supple and glistened in the early morning light streaming into the room through the closed curtains. Her body gleamed with perspiration, and yet she shivered. The black of her bra against her olive skin offered a contrast that captivated him. He arched her backwards and supported her on one arm. His other hand brushed delicately against her neck, making its way downwards, slowly, cherishing every inch of her skin. He paused at her breasts, then looking into her eyes, teased her, his fingers deliberating between them, before proceeding lower.

Not intending to be left behind, Lavanya tugged at his T-shirt and slid it up his chest. Shourya helped matters along by taking it off and dropping it on the floor. She pulled away from him and looked at his bare upper body in admiration. She leaned into him and kissed his chest, licking softly, running her tongue around in circles. It drove him crazy.

He ran his palms down her back, neck to waist, sliding smoothly over her silken skin. The only obstacle he encountered was the strap of her bra; it took him just a second to dispense with it. His hands moved to her front and held her supple mounds captive. He pushed her back on the bed and followed her down, sucking on her neck, biting her, all the while rubbing his fingers over the sensitive skin of her breasts. He nibbled on her chin, before running his tongue over it and licking a path downwards. Her fingernails dug into his back and she arched, moaning, as he sucked on her breasts. His lips and his tongue toyed with her like a master, responding to the way Lavanya's body throbbed at his touch. His hands skimmed down her waist to her hips. He pressed her to him, their desire now visible in the way their bodies clung to each other.

Shourya looked up at her, his mouth still feasting on her. Lavanya's body was quivering under his touch, her lips swollen. He looked into her eyes, hungry with desire and saw her eyes shine with tears.

'No. No crying,' he whispered, tucking a strand of hair that had fallen on her face behind her ear. Just inches away from her face, he noticed how pretty she looked when distressed.

'Shourya . . .' She was looking at him, clearly scared.

'It's okay.' Shourya leaned over her and planted a kiss on her forehead. He stayed there, breathing in the scent of her hair. She smelled so good, so familiar. Shourya felt his throat constrict, as the memory of her walking away that day at the airport without turning back one last time snuck into his mind. They had been through so much, but they had survived and found their way back to each other. After all this time. 'It's okay. This is me. You don't have to be scared, Lavanya, this is us. We are in this together.'

17

She had to stop this. She could not let him do this; she could not put him at risk. Shourya kissed her forehead again, and she breathed in the sweet scent of his body. Her hands were on his back, holding him close. But she had to let go. She knew she had to, yet her fingers still clutched his back.

Shourya was looking at her, his eyes dark with passion. He needed her. She could feel it in her body. She needed him too, more than she had ever needed anything.

Lavanya held his face in her hands and pulled him closer. He kissed her nose, and his hands caught both of hers and pinned them above her head. He kept them there, holding them prisoner with one of his hands, while the other started exploring again. His face was hidden in her hair, their cheeks touching. She could feel his breathing was troubled, but it was nowhere as bad as the condition she was in. But when his hands pulled at her pants. She cringed.

Before she could say anything, Shourya looked up. 'What is it?'

'I . . . *can't*,' she croaked.

Shourya was looking at her intently, and she was trying her best not to break down in front of him. She wanted to tell him. But it would ruin everything. He loved her. If she kept her secret to herself, she could pretend to have a bright future filled with love and happiness with him. But once she told him about her disease, everything would change. Knowing the kind of person he was, and how he felt about her, he would not be able to leave her and be happy in his life. He would stay with her. They would try to make it work, but what kind of life would that be, living with a time bomb, death dangling in front of her every second of every day?

And this was the best case scenario. Even though Shourya had told her that he did not have feelings for Deepti, Lavanya did not believe him completely. She did not think that he was lying to her but maybe he himself did not know the truth about how he actually felt. The past few weeks they spent together had been a whirlwind affair. It had left their lives upside-down.

'Lavanya, talk to me.' Shourya was studying her with such concern that she nearly broke down.

'I cannot do this . . .' she said, steeling herself. She was sad. She finally admitted to herself just how sad she was. The last few weeks had been testing. She was confused and scared and in love and dying. She wanted to hurt herself. She wanted to turn to drugs again. But it was that which had landed her in trouble in the first place. It wasn't an option any more. And then Shourya had come along. The one person she could always rely on, the one person who loved her despite all the shit she put him through, all the pain she caused him. He had made it easier, so much easier, without even knowing.

But now she could not afford the dream any more. She had to get back to reality.

'I'm sorry . . . I just . . . can't . . .' She pulled her hands from Shourya's grip and he let them loose.

He moved off her, and lay on his side, facing her. 'What's wrong?'

Lavanya pushed herself up against the head rest, reaching for the comforter while trying not to look directly at Shourya. She did not trust herself to stay away from him. He was everything she could not have. He was perfect. He was kind and funny and he loved her.

He had been her chance at a normal life.

Shourya pulled the comforter to her neck, covering her. His finger grazed her collarbone slightly, making her shiver. How would she let him go? How would she live without him?

'Lavanya, what is it? You are scaring me now. You can tell me. You know you can tell me *anything*,' he said. His eyes were pleading with hers, looking for answers.

'I . . . I am . . .'

'Nervous . . . ? Is that what this is?' Shourya was inspecting her closely.

Lavanya did not meet his eyes at first, but when he persisted, she had to look up. *She could not do it.* She could not find words. She could not end this fantasy, not so soon. She nodded.

'You don't have to be. This is me. There's nothing to be nervous about,' Shourya said earnestly. Even though he was serious, she could see a smile creeping to his face.

She would give herself another moment of fantasy, and then she would tell him. *Just one day*, she reasoned. It could be one more thing—perhaps the most important thing—on her wish list. She cleared her throat and said, 'Why do I get the feeling that you are enjoying this?'

He burst out laughing as soon as she said it.

'That is so mean. You are so mean, Shourya Kapoor!'

'I might be, but I'm not being mean right now. You're just hilarious. You should've seen your expression. You scared me. If you're not ready, and you need more time or it's too soon, all you had to do is say the word.'

'That's what I did,' Lavanya said.

'No. What you did was freak me out completely. Do you have any idea what kind of thoughts came into my mind? Judging by the expression on your face, I thought something was seriously wrong.' Shourya shook his head at her.

She let him laugh at her. She laughed with him too. Who knew how many more such moments they would get to share?

'What? I was just nervous,' she grumbled.

'Just nervous. You were behaving like a scared virgin! I thought this was the first time you . . .' Shourya froze mid-sentence at the expression on her face. 'You . . . *are*!'

Lavanya felt the blood rush to her cheeks and she hastily looked down at her hands. Her nails were uneven and ugly, and she tore at them out of habit. She did not know where to look.

'Shit,' Shourya muttered. 'I didn't mean to be insensitive. I was just kidding. I don't know why I thought that was funny. It was a really bad joke. God. I'm such an asshole—'

'Shut up.'

'I'm sorry.'

'Shut *up*.'

He shut up. He could not look at her either, his eyes were darting around the room, jumping from one subdued, beige hotel-room object to another. She found that endearing. Shourya had a wonderful sense of humour and very rarely apologized for anything he said or did. Mostly because the man rarely did any wrong to anyone. It was unusual to see him embarrassed, and Lavanya enjoyed every minute of it.

'I am sleepy,' Lavanya said. She picked up his T-shirt from the floor and put it on. Slipping back under the covers, she adjusted a pillow under her head.

'I really am sorry,' Shourya said.

'I know.' Lavanya turned to her side, facing away from Shourya and reached for his hand. 'Come. *Sleep* with me.'

Shourya obeyed promptly. He lay down next to her and sliding his hand around her stomach, he held her from behind. Lavanya curved her body to fit into his. He rested his head over hers, and when he whispered 'I love you so much' in her ear, she could do nothing but close her eyes.

~

'Deepti?'

Shourya heard the name, and was suddenly wide awake. Lavanya was still curled up next to him, asleep. The room was dark; he estimated it was late evening. They had slept through the day. There was no one else in the room.

Then who—?

He was the one who had called out.

He gently extricated his arm from under Lavanya's neck, careful not to wake her up. Why had he called out Deepti's name? It was a dream, he realized—a dream in which he was back in California and she was leaving Avik for him.

Why was he dreaming of her all of a sudden?

Shourya got out of bed hastily and went to his room in the suite. He found his cell phone lying on the side table next to the bed. Sure enough, there were new messages from her. She had been texting him repeatedly, making sure she was never far from his thoughts. And now his dreams.

Or was there something more to it?

He could not answer that question. He loved Lavanya deeply. He knew that. He had always loved her, even when she was far away, even when he had hated her. And now, by some twist of fate, they had come back into each other's lives, they had been given another chance, and this time, she loved him too.

It felt as if he was living a dream. *His* dream, from years ago.

Then why was Deepti occupying a space in *this* dream? Was his subconscious trying to tell him something?

This was Lavanya. She was the best person he knew. And she deserved more than this. She deserved undivided love from the person she gave her love to. Shourya knew he could not be true to her till he figured things out with Deepti. He had been telling himself for months that he did not love her any more, that it was only what she'd done—the cheating, the lying, the betraying—that he could not get over. But what if it was not true? What if there was something more that he was missing?

Maybe he was panicking more than he needed to, but *this was Lavanya*. He could not do anything that would hurt her. If he rushed into something that he couldn't handle and she got hurt in the process . . . he could not have that. He had assumed the responsibility of taking care of her ten years ago. He could not be the one to hurt her. He had to leave. He had to figure things out, find a way out of his mess. Escaping from his life and finding refuge outside of it was not the solution—it was only a way to clear his head. He could not go on like that forever. He knew he had to return some day. But unless he sorted out things, he could not let Lavanya invest her feelings in him.

He looked for flights back to Delhi and booked the one that left the earliest. He also called the airline he scheduled to fly back to the US on and requested a flight on an earlier date. Sneaking away behind her back and leaving her there was an awful thing to do, but he saw no other way out of this. It was better to hurt her a little now than a lot later.

He put on another shirt—Lavanya was wearing the one he had on that morning—and collected his things from around the room. He stuffed everything in his overnighter. Before leaving, he went to Lavanya's room and left a note under the door. He could have just texted her, but a handwritten note felt like the lesser of two evils.

He did not want to leave. It was only because he cared about her more than he cared about himself that he was doing this. It was the only way he could ensure that he was not pulling her into something they weren't ready for . . . even though it felt like he had been waiting for it to happen all his life. Everything with Lavanya had happened too fast. She was not equipped to take care of herself; she had never been, so he had to look after her. Now he had to decide if he was good enough for his best friend.

18

Lavanya was woken up by the sound of a door closing. It was dark; she did not where she was or what she was doing there. Then it came to her, slowly. Yesterday . . . He loved her . . . The memories brought a smile to her face. She could smell him, but when she reached out to the other side of the bed, it was cold and empty.

Her fingers searched for the bedside lamp. When the soft yellow glow spread through the room, a chill ran over her skin. The empty room did not just feel empty; it felt deserted. She knew instantly that something was not right.

Lavanya pushed the covers aside and jumped out of the bed. Her feet landed on the clothes she had discarded on the carpeted floor in the morning. She was still wearing Shourya's white shirt. Maybe that was why she could still smell him. As she pulled open the door, she found a piece of paper lying under it, one side jagged, indicating that it had been taken out of a spiral bound notepad.

And just like that, she *knew*.

Her knees buckled, and she slumped to the floor, her back propped against the wall. She stared at the note, signed S. She did not have to read it to know that he was gone.

~

Lavanya did not take the flight back to Delhi right away. She stayed in Goa for three more days, walking barefoot on the beaches in Arambol village. She was there when the sun rose, she was there when it was at its peak, its heat burning her skin, and she was there when it set, making way for the cool evening breeze. She saw women in bikinis sunbathing, kids running around in cute little swimsuits, chasing each other and building castles in the sand. There were grand parties happening on New Year's Eve in the clubs lining the beach. Lavanya sat on the sand and looked on, hearing only the shrieks of people in the distance who were clearly intoxicated.

All that time, she only wondered one thing—where could she run to from here?

That was the one thing she knew how to do. But she could find no place to run to this time. She had already left behind her life at New York and come to Delhi. Once there, she had avoided dealing with her parents by spending all her time with Shourya, and when he was not there, with Toughy. Then she had escaped all the way to Goa. But now that Shourya had left her, she was faced with hours and days alone, when she had nothing to do but think—about him, about her parents, about her disease. She reached the conclusion that she could no longer keep her secret to herself. Her mind made up, she marshalled whatever strength she could and took a flight back to Delhi. She found herself at the doorstep of her family home, a few hours later. She knocked on the door, before remembering she had a key.

Lavanya set down her small duffel bag on the porch and rummaged through her handbag for the keys. She found it strange that the porch lights hadn't been turned on. It was almost 11 p.m., and their neighbourhood was the kind that became quiet shortly after the sun set. The first week of

January tended to be the coldest of the year, so Lavanya was not surprised to find her fingers frozen. From the silence that enveloped the house, she assumed her parents were asleep and tried not to make any noise as she turned the key in the lock. Pushing the door open softly, she carried her bag inside and had just placed it on the floor when she heard Toughy's excited bark. She turned around to see the puppy tottering to her, his lack of one leg not slowing him down in the least.

Lavanya dropped to her knees and welcomed Toughy into her arms. He felt small and warm and soft against her chest. The way he eagerly licked her face and his whole rear-end shook from his furious tail-wagging, made her eyes fill with tears. The feeling of being so loved and cherished tugged at her heart.

Shourya had told her that he loved her, then why had he left her? Lavanya stroked Toughy's smooth dark fur, as he looked up at her with his beautiful, black eyes. The upstairs light turned on, and in the next moment, Lavanya saw her mother descend the stairs.

'Lavi?' she said, her voice unsure.

'Yeah, Mom.' Two words, and already her tears were spilling over. She did not try to stop them. 'Mumma.'

'What—?'

Years of pent-up emotion welling up inside, Lavanya walked towards her mother, who was stumbling about in the dark, clearly sleepy. Her mother looked startled at first, and even more so when Lavanya reached for her hands and held them tightly between hers. Big fat tears were rolling down her cheeks, but thankfully, her body didn't give her away.

'Lavi? What is wrong?' her mother asked. She was wearing a long dark-brown nightgown, with flowers all over. In the darkness, Lavanya could see only one side of her face clearly. 'Are you okay?'

'No . . .' Lavanya said. 'I am not okay, Mumma . . . I am tired of pretending I am fine . . . I can't any more . . .' Lavanya broke down. She hadn't called her mother Mumma since she was a little kid. At that moment, in the dark, defeated, she felt like a child again, needing her Mumma to protect her and tell her that everything would be okay.

Her mother looked confused at first, but as the remnants of sleep left her, her eyes became sharp and piercing.

'Lavi . . .'

Lavanya pulled her mother to the living room and made her sit on the oversized green couch. She clasped her weathered hands in her own, and said, 'I don't know how to tell you . . . I don't think I should. But, it's wrong . . . you not knowing . . .'

'What are you talking about?' Lavanya felt her mother's grip on her hand loosen. She could see her eyes narrow and her lips tighten into a thin line.

'Mom,' Lavanya bowed her head.

She did not know how to begin. She could not tell her mother about the affair that her husband had had years ago. Lavanya had never forgiven her father for it, and she had still not moved on. And in the process of getting her father out of her life, she had also left her mother behind. What right did she have now to come back years later and turn her mother's life upside down? What good would that do?

She was home now, but she didn't know for how long. Her disease would eventually kill her, and she would leave her mother behind, once again. Only this time, with nothing, not even her husband.

This was not the time for that. If she wanted her mother to know, she should have said something years ago. Now, it would only wreck her, her family, her life.

'I know.'

Lavanya barely heard her mother's whisper. 'What?' she gasped.

'I know about the affair . . . your father's . . . I have known for a long time,' her mother said, looking straight ahead, her voice calm and composed.

'You knew? How . . . when?'

'Your father and I were in a bad place for most parts of that year. It was difficult, complicated. And then when this . . . this *thing* happened, I knew something was wrong. I didn't know what at the time but I suspected something was going on,' she exhaled loudly, as if trying to gather the strength to continue. 'You suddenly started acting strange, and I got distracted with that. I thought it was something related to boys, or drugs even. But Shourya was there, and he always looked after you—that reassured me somewhat. You and your father . . . it was like one day you woke up and decided to pretend he did not exist. Just like that. You would not talk to him, you would not look at me . . . you did not even want to be in the same room as him. Nobody told me what was going on, and soon, it was time for you to go, and that . . . It was hard . . .'

Lavanya gulped. She was not crying any more. For the first time, she was seeing her mother's side of things. She had had no idea.

Her mother went on, 'All my energies went into trying to act like everything was okay. It was a wonderful thing, you getting accepted to Harvard, your dream . . . but it was hard for me. It did not feel like you were going abroad to study, it felt like you were . . . *leaving*. And then, the day came, and you left, and what I feared the most happened. We heard from you less and less each week, and you grew distant with every conversation.'

Lavanya saw her cringe. Her face looked smaller, more tired and pained, as she said, 'It felt like we had lost you, our only daughter. That's when your father told me . . . a few weeks after you left. It was difficult. Even now, when I think of those months . . . those were the hardest days of my life. The darkest. I did not think life would ever be normal again, that I would be okay again. But he was there, every day, trying to make it better. He apologized to me, he told me everything—that the affair had lasted a week, and that you'd found out about it. I never thought I would be able to forgive him. But you know what? What we had was bigger than that. He was my husband, we had been together for twenty years, and I could not throw it all away because of one mistake. A mistake he confessed to making, and tried to make up for . . . still does, every single day since . . .'

'Mom, he cheated on you. How could you—?' Lavanya could not make sense of what her mother was saying.

'Nobody is perfect, Lavi. We have all made mistakes. It's what we decide to do about them that matters. I cannot let one mistake define our relationship. It was difficult to forgive him, I won't deny that . . . it was a long journey but we took it together.'

'If you knew . . . When you found out and all this was happening, why didn't you tell me?'

'You had already left. And I suppose I needed time to process things. When your father and I were finally in a better place, I wanted to talk to you. I came very close to calling you several times, but just because I could find it in my heart to forgive him, it didn't mean that I could ask the same of you. And I thought it would do us all some good to bury it in the past. I hoped that time would resolve the discord between you and your father, that when you came back during holidays, things would be . . . different.'

'But I never came home—' Lavanya exhaled.

'I do not blame you for anything, Lavi. What he did is not something that should be acceptable behaviour. I probably do not have a say in what you decide to do. But . . . it's been seven years, beta. He is a good man. He has done everything he can for our family. I know you want to hate him, maybe that is easier for you than resolving this, but he loves you. He cares about you, and . . . I know it kills him that he is dead to his own daughter.'

At a loss for words, Lavanya looked at Toughy. He was lying on the floor between her feet, nuzzling her toes every now and then as if to offer strength and support, as if he could sense what she was going through. She could feel her mother's eyes on her, but she was too ashamed to look up her. She bent down instead and scratched Toughy's belly, which he took as an invitation to crawl on to her lap and curl up.

She had left home when her family was going through its biggest crisis. She wished her mother would say something. The silence was killing her.

They sat quietly for a long time, absorbing everything, before her mother said softly, 'I know he still has not forgiven himself. He can't. Not until *you* forgive him.'

Lavanya nodded slowly and looked her mother straight in the eye. 'Can you call him, Mom?'

Her mother's face relaxed, and a single teardrop escaped the corner of one eye.

Lavanya gulped. 'I have to tell you both something.'

~

Shourya got into his car and put on his sunglasses. It was a sunny morning, but it was windy outside. The bright blue sky was just an illusion; he could see clouds approaching with the wind. The forecast said there was a thirty per cent chance of precipitation. Shourya thought it would rain before lunch.

He missed Lavanya. No matter how hard he tried to distract himself, he ended up thinking about her and the time they had spent together the past month. So far, the New Year had sucked. It had kicked off with the eighteen-hour journey from New Delhi to San Francisco, which had left him terribly jet lagged. When he reached the apartment, only Avik was home; Deepti was missing. Shourya hadn't thought much of it, till the next day, when as soon as he stepped out of his bedroom, Avik accused him of stealing his girlfriend. Shourya found it so outrageous, he burst out laughing. Avik did not seem to appreciate it, and showered him with abuses. It only made Shourya laugh harder. It was quite hilarious, the whole situation, now that Shourya had had time away from it to think about it. It turned out that Deepti and Avik were 'taking a break', and she had moved in with one of her girlfriends in the meantime. These people were crazy. The encounter with Avik had only strengthened his resolve to find and move into a place of his own as soon as possible. Unfortunately, he soon realized, it wasn't that easy. It took him the better part of three days and several house viewings to find an apartment that he liked and put a deposit on it. Sadly, the place would not be available for two weeks, which meant he had to share the apartment with Avik.

Rather than focus on that, he concentrated his energies on getting himself transferred to Boston, which would take him closer to Lavanya. If everything worked out well, he knew Lavanya would want him close enough to drive over on weekends.

When she heard he was back, Deepti called Shourya and said she wanted to meet him. He was not so sure about being sucked into that madness again, but she insisted. Thinking it could be the only way to find out where they stood, Shourya had agreed to meet her.

That's where he was headed that morning. They were meeting in an outdoor restaurant called Jupiter, a brewpub they used to frequent on special occasions when they were dating. He had taken her there once on her birthday, and they had celebrated one of their anniversaries there—the last one.

As he parked his car and got out, he realized he was more excited at the prospect of the wood-fired pizzas than meeting Deepti. *God!* He missed Lavanya.

He had made a pact with himself to not call Lavanya till he had figured everything out and was absolutely sure. Through all the madness of house-hunting and the drama with Avik, he had just about managed not to give in to temptation and call Lavanya. But he was getting more and more assured with every minute. This was the final test—meeting Deepti.

As he walked towards the restaurant, he could see her sitting inside. She got up when she saw him, and came forward to hug him when he got closer. Her hair smelled like it always had, of grapefruit and ginger, but unlike before, he found the smell too sweet this time.

'How have you been?' she asked, clutching his arm. She was looking up at him with her cat eyes, lined thickly with deep brown eyeliner, pulled at the ends to make her look even more catty. She was wearing a blue dress that they had shopped for together. He had been desperate to go home, but she had coaxed him into visiting another store—the last one, she promised—where she wanted to try on one more dress. His heart had skipped a beat and he had fallen a little more in love with her when she had come out of the trial room wearing the blue dress. Now, however, when he saw her in it, he felt absolutely nothing. Not even nostalgia.

He had his answer. They hadn't even spoken yet, but he was already sure that he had no romantic feelings left for Deepti. The memories of the time they had spent together, the ones that haunted him for the better part of a year, now felt distant.

'Hey, Deepti,' he said.

'Why are you smiling?' she asked, smiling nervously herself.

He shrugged his shoulders. 'I have no idea. I'm just . . . happy, I guess.'

'Yeah? About meeting me?'

She was looking at him apprehensively. He did not want to break her heart. Before it had ended badly, their relationship had been mostly good. For several years, she had been the person closest to him, the person he loved and cared about the most. Maybe it had all been a lie, but a part of him was oddly thankful to her for cheating on him, for breaking his heart and chucking their relationship into the drain. Had that not happened, he would never have found his way back to Lavanya.

Shourya had to tell Deepti that it was over. Their relationship had run its course, and it could not be revived. And if she took it well, maybe he would tell her about Lavanya too. If nothing else, it would help her accept that they weren't meant to be, and move on. Maybe she would wish him well. And maybe one day she could be happy for him.

19

Lavanya had nowhere to run. This time, she did not want to. The situation between her father and her was twisted. It had been complicated to begin with, and over the years, it had become something much bigger than she could handle. Her heart felt like it would jump out of her mouth as she sat in the dark, holding on to Toughy while she waited for her mother to wake up her father and bring him down.

She heard the door of their bedroom open, and a second later, the staircase was illuminated softly by the light coming from the room. Lavanya could hear muffled sounds, and then, a few minutes later, she saw them come down the stairs, her mother leading the way.

Lavanya forced herself to look at her father's face, and keep looking. That she had been so stubborn and unforgiving for years together that she could not find it in her heart to even spare her own father a glance made her feel ashamed of herself. It had gone on long enough. She had to end it.

He was looking at her, and she met his eye. Years ago, there was a time when she had looked at that face adoringly every day, when he had been her superhero. The girl from all those years ago was still inside her. She could still see the father she had loved and respected in the face that had aged a decade since the last time she saw him. She was surprised to find that despite having been woken up in the middle of the night, his eyes were strangely alert. His daughter wanted to talk to him, and it seemed to have shocked him enough to wake him up completely. Lavanya wanted to laugh and cry at the same time.

Her father looked from her to her mother questioningly, but did not say anything.

'Dad, I'm sorry,' she said before she lost her courage. She was still sitting, with Toughy on her lap. She felt safer like that, having the dog as a shield.

'Why are you . . .?' her father's voice came out deep and low. He cleared his throat. 'You don't have anything to apologize for. I do. I never got a chance . . .'

'I never gave you a chance,' Lavanya insisted. 'I should not have left home like that. Should not have cut you both out of my life. Mom, I am so sorry. I never meant for you to get hurt like that. I was selfish, I was only thinking about myself. I left everything behind. Everyone.'

She bit her lip to contain her tears. Things could have been so different, so much better if she had had the strength to have this conversation back then. She would not have been lonely. She would not have been dealing with depression alone, and resorted to drugs. No matter how much she had tried to blame everything going wrong in her life on her father, she didn't truly believe it. It was she who had to bear the responsibility for where she was in her life, what she was dealing with.

'Lavi, beta, I never meant for you or your mother to get hurt,' her father said. He was sitting next to her in his flannel pyjamas and an old full-sleeved T-shirt. He did not feel as big next to her as he used to, when she was younger. He smelled like . . . Dad. His hands were resting in his lap and he was scratching his fingernails. As Lavanya looked, small bits of his nails fell to the floor. She could feel his nervousness, and realized it should not be like that. A father should not have to be anxious around his daughter. And in that moment, she felt a warmth spread in her chest and a heart get lighter as she finally let it go—her anger, her fear, her grudge, everything.

'I have been so asham—'

'No, Dad, no. Please don't. I know how you feel. Mom told me everything,' Lavanya stopped him. It was enough that they had taken their first steps to becoming father and daughter again. She had forgiven him and he did not hold anything against her either. She could not watch him grovel in front of her. She could not do that to her father. If anything, she cursed herself for not doing this sooner instead of now, when they did not have much time left.

She leaned on his shoulder quietly, and he reached out and patted her arm. There, in that moment, it was enough. It was all they needed.

But it was not over. Far from it. She had to tell them about her disease. She could not keep them in the dark any more. If they had only a limited number of days left with their daughter, they deserved to know.

She wanted nothing more than to break down and dissolve into a puddle of tears. She was losing courage with every second, seeing her mother standing at the door, her face partially covered with her hand as she cried, happy and sad. She did not have the heart to turn it all into sadness.

But when her mother came forward and asked her what she wanted to tell them, Lavanya knew it was time.

'I . . .' her voice got caught. She cleared her throat, and said clearly, one word after another, almost mechanically. 'I have HIV.'

Her announcement was greeted with a moment of deathly quiet and then all hell broke loose. She heard her mother panic, and let out a yelp. She saw her father's eyes widen and his chest heave. They were shaking her, asking her for details. She told them that all lawyers did coke in New York. She did not tell them she was depressed. She did not blame them, or anyone else for what happened to her and where she was. It was refreshing to accept responsibility. It was agonising to see her mother dissolve into her father's arms and weep.

She felt Toughy lick her hand and she held on to him tightly as she answered their questions about her disease. It felt odd to accept it, as if saying it out loud made it even more real.

By the time they went to sleep again—at least try—it was nearly dawn. All the tears and lack of sleep over the last few days was taking a toll on Lavanya. Her head was aching, her body was fatigued, her brain was numb and her heart was broken.

~

Lavanya, flanked on either side by her parents, sat opposite Dr Meera Shah. They had been up all night, interrogating her. When did it happen, how did it happen, how long had she known, what did the doctor say, what treatment she was getting. They were aghast when she told them she had not seen the doctor yet and that she did not know what her test results meant, and apart from knowing she was HIV positive, she did not know anything else about her disease, but she was convinced that she had AIDS. She did not tell her parents that part, though. She did not want to burden them, not till it was confirmed.

After a quick breakfast, her parents had dragged Lavanya to AIIMS and waited with her at the reception. Dr Shah was notified, and they were told that she had an opening in one hour and forty minutes. They did not speak to each other the entire time they waited outside the doctor's office. It was only when they were called inside and they took seats across the table from the doctor that one of them spoke.

'What does this mean, Doctor?' her father asked.

'Is she going to be okay?' her mother added, her voice unstable.

Lavanya felt like she would throw up. She could see the pain she was causing to her parents, and she felt terrible about it. No parents should have to experience the agony of watching their child die. She wished she could go back a day, and keep pretending she was okay. Maybe if she ran away from her disease long enough, she would outrun it.

But admitting that she had it, saying it out loud, telling her parents—it had all made it real. Tangible. She was already on an accelerated journey towards her death, and there was no stopping that train.

'I was waiting for you,' Dr Shah said, pulling down her spectacles and examining Lavanya over them. 'We made several calls to you, but never received a response.'

Lavanya nodded. Dr Shah was holding a copy of her test results. All Lavanya could do was stare at that.

'When I was told earlier today that you were here, I went through your reports again. I will discuss them with you in a moment. But first, Lavanya, I have to talk to you about something. Do I have your attention?' Dr Shah asked.

Lavanya nodded again. Her mother clutched her hand, perhaps in the hope of steadying her and providing support. But her mother's own hand was shaking even more violently than Lavanya's. They held on anyway, giving and receiving strength.

'Good,' Dr Shah continued. She laid down the documents she was holding and said, 'Look, Lavanya, you have to realize that this is serious, okay? Having HIV is a severe illness. We have to do our very best, everything we can, to control it.

We have to create a treatment plan, based on these results and your situation, and we have to stick to it very strictly. And we have to meet regularly, for check-ups, to see how you are responding to the treatment and make changes in your drugs and regime whenever needed. I know it is hard, and it is a lot to wrap your head around. But for us to fight this, you have to first accept the situation. I need to know that you understand all this, and you will do everything you have to in order to get things under control.'

'She will,' her father said determinedly.

Lavanya felt shattered. She was not sure she could handle it. Her mother squeezed her hand.

Dr Shah looked from Lavanya to her father. 'That's great to know,' she said, and picked up the reports. She began. 'Well. It was fortunate that you were diagnosed early. These reports confirm what I told you the last time we met. You are in the second phase of HIV infection, which is clinical latency. At this point, the virus is active and reproducing, though at a very low pace. The game plan here is to restrict that growth as much as we can. I will need to sit down with two of my colleagues and devise a treatment plan for you. That is, of course, if you want to get your treatment from us. Most people choose to get a second opinion before deciding. Also, it says in your file that you are a resident of New York, so before we build a team and work on your treatment plan, we will need to know your decision.'

'Wait . . . Doctor . . .' Lavanya said, once Dr Shah stopped speaking. Her brain tried to process the information she had been given. She shivered as she spoke slowly, 'Does that . . . do you mean I *don't* have AIDS?'

'No. Of course not. Didn't we discuss that the last time around? I thought I told you that you were in the second phase.'

'Yeah, you did. But you said it was an estimate based on how long it had been since I got infected. You said we would know only once I got the tests done,' Lavanya was tripping over her words, the next one rushing to get out before the first. Her whole body had become warm and she felt the palms of her hands leave her mother's skin wet.

'I did. And after looking at the results, I can confirm that.'

'I don't have AIDS.' Lavanya breathed out.

'Yes, you don't. In fact, you're in a very early stage of phase two. Patients have had long lives when taken proper care of. You have to be very alert, of course. Apart from the treatment, which will have to continue throughout your life, you have to take precautions, make changes to your lifestyle. You have to accept that this is going to be a part of you. And then we . . .'

Lavanya had stopped listening. She let out a long, tortured breath and sat back in the chair. She could not believe it was happening. She was not dying. Maybe not for a long time. Who knows? Maybe she even had a chance at a normal life. There would be several complications, but they would handle them. It was a small price to pay in exchange for her life.

Her mother was hugging her, and her father was talking to the doctor, and she let out a nervous laugh. There were tears in her eyes, but they were not flowing. Maybe there won't be more tears any more. Maybe life would get better.

~

Shourya paced his apartment, running his hand through his head. Why wasn't she taking his calls? He must have called her fifty times in twelve hours. Could it be that she was mad because he had abandoned her in Goa, leaving her with nothing but a note as an explanation? It was a good enough reason.

After meeting with Deepti, Shourya had recognized how far along he had come. She felt like something from a long time ago. He had expected to be angry; he had been furious with her and around her every time he had met her since their break up. But he was surprised to find that he was not. He had realized he was over her, that she had become a part of his past. More than anything, he accepted that he was in love with Lavanya, that she was his present and future and no one else mattered.

He dialled her number again. Even if she had decided to stay back in Goa and taken the flight they had booked beforehand, she ought to be back in Delhi by then. Then why was her phone going straight to voicemail?

He contemplated calling her home. But what if she had already left for New York? Maybe that was it. She could be on a flight back to the US, or fighting jet lag or something. He had been up all night, calling her in India, but if she was in New York, the time difference is only three hours. Maybe she was asleep. That could explain it.

He tried to believe that reasoning, but couldn't. It could be that she was infuriated at him and never wanted to talk to him again. He cursed himself. He should have called her sooner. But he couldn't have. He had to be absolutely sure before he did anything further. He had not meant to hurt her in the process. But it wouldn't be wrong of her to be angry with the man who confessed his love for her and then left her alone in a town hundreds of miles from home, with a note. *That note.* He wanted to kick himself. Why did he think it was a good idea? It was just stupid.

Not able to control himself, he finally dialled the Suryavanshis' home number. He made up his mind to just ask casually about how things were. He didn't want to cause trouble or raise concern in case Lavanya wasn't there. It was almost midnight in India, but the phone was picked up before he could disconnect.

Mrs Suryavanshi greeted, 'Hello?'

'Oh, Aunty. Hello! This is Shourya.' He realized he was whispering, even though it was broad daylight in California and there was nobody around. He spoke louder, 'I am sorry; I didn't realize what time it is there.'

'Shourya! *Beta*, is Lavanya there? Wait—she can't be already, can she? What time is it there?'

'A little after ten in the morning. I'm back in the US now. Lavanya isn't here . . .' He was confused.

'I know that you went back. Lavanya is on her way there to see you. Something about a note and your gall at having given it to her. She didn't seem happy about it. Didn't she tell you she was coming?'

Shourya burst into laughter, suddenly releasing all the tension from his body that had kept him on edge ever since he had left Goa. 'No. No, she didn't tell me she was coming here. I guess she was counting on the element of surprise.'

20

Now that Lavanya was at his doorstep, she felt lost. Her hand was raised, knuckles about to knock on the door, when she paused. What if he didn't want her there?

When Dr Shah had told her she had time, her disease was at a manageable stage, the first thing she had done was tell her parents that she loved Shourya. Her mother was not surprised, and even though it did come as a shock to her father, she knew he had always approved of Shourya.

She only waited long enough for her doctors to work on her treatment regime. Once they did, they put her on it, and assigned her drugs and a timetable. She got on to the first flight she could find to San Francisco and boarded it, promising her parents that she would return soon.

She had not taken into account the eighteen hours she would have to spend in the air. The first flight, New Delhi to Tokyo, was eight hours long. Thankfully, she slept through most of it and time passed by easily. It was the three-hour layover at Tokyo airport and the ten-hour-long flight to SF following that that almost killed her. Time had come to a standstill. She couldn't sleep, couldn't eat, couldn't even concentrate on her movie or book. It was torture.

She thought of a hundred different scenarios, painted pictures in her mind of how the confrontation with Shourya would pan out. But all those hours of thinking had not prepared her for the actual event.

She dug around her sweatshirt pocket for his note and fished it out. It was crumpled; she must've read it a thousand times.

I love you. But you deserve better, I think. I mean you deserve better than me for sure, no doubt about that, but there's a chance I could be good enough too. I want to find out. I don't know what I'm saying. Sorry for ditching you like this though. But Goa is fun. Have a happy new year. I'll make this thing as quick as possible. And then, let's see. Maybe we could be something. I do love you. Bye, S.

What the hell did that even mean? Every time she read it, her fury mounted. It was not like Shourya to be confused. She did not even understand what exactly he was confused about.

She knocked on the door. If nothing else, she could at least find out what the stupid note actually meant. She knocked again.

A tall, skinny guy with a huge red pimple on his right cheek, just above a hideous goatee opened the door. 'Yes?' he questioned. He looked annoyed at the intrusion. Maybe it was the incessant knocking.

'Hey. You must be Avik. Is Shourya here?' Lavanya asked.

'I don't think—'

'Lavanya?' came a voice from behind the lanky guy.

She stepped in, to find Shourya coming out of a room, towards her. Avik rolled his eyes and went inside, to what Lavanya assumed was his room.

'Shourya Kapoor,' she muttered.

'Lavanya . . .' He was wearing a navy blue T-shirt with the words 'Peace, Love & Metal' written across his chest in white. It was late at night, and he looked like he had been woken up by the knocks on the door. She was making a habit of waking people up in the middle of the night.

He came and stood right in front of her, and her legs, as always, went weak. She barely managed to stay upright. It was all she could do to not reach out and hold his arm.

'The note,' she said.

'What?'

'Yeah. What the fuck was that thing?' she pushed it into his face. 'What am I supposed to make of this?'

'Whoa! Easy. I was just trying to figure things out. That was what I said. I love you, but I wanted to figure out if I was good enough for you. That's it.'

'Oh, is it? Read this and tell me if this makes sense.'

Shourya took the crumpled sheet of paper from her. After a moment, he said, 'Yeah. Yeah, that was pretty stupid, wasn't it?'

Lavanya almost smiled, and then checked herself. 'So, what does it mean? Have you figured it out yet?'

Shourya wasn't being funny, he wasn't saying anything light-hearted. In fact, he was being sincere. He looked serious. He was not smiling. It scared her.

'I only wanted to make sure I was being true to you. That there was nothing between me and Deepti. Because you deserve someone who will devote his everything to make you happ—'

'Yeah, yeah,' Lavanya cut him off. 'Tell me. What did you decide? Do you still love her?' Her stomach felt queasy. *He still loved Deepti, didn't he?* She knew it. She knew there was still something there.

Shourya took another step towards her, covering the rest of the distance between them. He cupped her face in his palms and looked into her eyes. Lavanya's heart was beating out of her mouth. As she gazed into his piercing eyes, she felt she would stop breathing any second.

'Do you still love her?' she croaked. Her legs had completely given up by then. If Shourya let go of her, she would fall to the ground.

'Lavanya Suryavanshi,' Shourya said, his breaths shallow. 'Ever since I left you in that hotel room and came here . . . all I've thought about is you.'

There. Just like that.

Lavanya wrapped her arms around him and nestled her face in the crook of his neck. 'For a minute there . . . you scared me,' she muttered into his skin.

His hands were around her waist, securing her in his arms. 'I love you,' he said, his voice gruff.

'I love you,' she said. She wanted to stay there forever, eyes closed, breathing in his scent, protected in his embrace. But she had not forgotten that she had something to tell him. It was time. She dropped her arms to his waist and tried to pull back. 'I have to tell you something.'

He let her go back a step, but still held her by her waist. 'I know,' he said.

'You know . . . that I have to tell you something?' Lavanya asked, confused.

'I know what you have to tell me.'

How? How did people already know things when she was on the verge of confessing? First her mother, now Shourya. She was confused. There was no way he could know.

'What . . . do you . . . Do you mean you know that I have—'

'HIV? Yes. I know,' Shourya said and pulled her back into his arms.

~

Shourya held her close to his chest. He could feel her resisting, but he needed this hug. Ever since she had found out about her HIV, he had not been able to think about anything else. He was in shock. It refused to leave his mind even for a second.

'How do you know? When did you find out?' Lavanya asked, speaking into his T-shirt, her voice stifled.

'Today morning. You were on the flight here. I had called your home. Aunty told me. Lavanya, why didn't you tell me before?' Shourya finally set her at arm's-length as he spoke.

'I thought you would hate me.' Lavanya spoke quietly, not looking at him.

'No. *What?* Of course not! I could never hate you. Why would you think that?'

'Because I hate myself.'

'Lavanya, no. I am worried about you, I cannot believe this is happening to us, and I am scared of losing you . . . I am scared to death . . . but I don't hate you. How can you think that? Don't ever think that.' He could feel Lavanya's body tremble beneath his hands.

'I am scared too.'

'It will be okay. It will be all right,' he said quickly. When Mrs Suryavanshi had told him about their meeting with the doctor, Shourya's world had stopped. He couldn't believe that he had spent the last month with Lavanya but failed to notice that she was dealing with something as big and terrifying as HIV. All by herself. 'You should've told me. Why didn't you tell me?'

'What good would that have done? I thought I was dying. And I thought you would go back to your life and forget about me. I didn't want to be the reason you got hurt again. My death wouldn't have affected you if you were far away . . .'

'Like hell it wouldn't have. God. Do you not know *anything* about me? I can't even think about . . . If anything were to happen to you . . .' his voice got caught. Just thinking about something happening to Lavanya felt like someone was constricting his throat. 'Never say something like that . . .'

Lavanya nodded. 'I'm sorry.'

'Don't think like that. I'm here now, I am with you. Your dad sent over all the reports to me and the treatment regime. I am getting a second opinion from a specialist here. We will find the best treatment for you. I'm going to take care of you.'

Mr Suryavanshi had told him all about Lavanya's treatment plan. He said that her team was positive about it, and that there was no cause for panic, as long as she was under the treatment and her condition was monitored on schedule. After the phone call, Shourya had spent most of the day at his computer, researching HIV and finding out as much as he could. He made calls to hospitals that specialized in providing treatment to HIV patients, and found an article about a study that said now in America the average HIV patient lived longer than people who did not have HIV. It is so because they take such good care of their health, that they avoid the usual severe problems like cardiac arrests and hypertension. Shourya would make sure Lavanya was one of them. He wouldn't let anything happen to her.

A big part of him still had not been able to digest the information. Twelve hours were not nearly enough to process something of this magnitude. He was terrified inside. He deserved some kind of a medal of valour for putting up a strong front before Lavanya. One of them had to be strong, and given that she was the one dealing with HIV, had been dealing with it alone till now, he had to step up. He had to be strong for her.

'I don't want to die.'

Her voice was so low, it barely reached him. He hated how miserable she sounded. 'Everyone dies. Today, or fifty years from now. What does it matter?' he said in a low, sincere tone.

Lavanya looked confused for a second. 'Are you saying you don't care if I die——?' Her brows knit in concentration.

Shourya had always found that adorable about her. 'Oh, wait. Did you just quote *Troy* to me?'

'You will never be lovelier than you are now. We'll never be here again.'

'Seriously! Stop with the *Troy* quotes!'

Shourya chuckled.

'God. Talk about poor timing.'

But she was smiling, a smile that slowly bloomed into laughter. Shourya joined in, and they both laughed loudly at the absurdity of his timing. They laughed as if there was nothing wrong in their lives any more, as if everything was suddenly okay, or they did not care if it wasn't. And then, in that moment, he knew . . . together, they could move mountains.

Shourya pulled Lavanya to his chest, and silenced her laugh with a kiss. His lips brushed against her, and his thumb stroked her collarbone. She wrapped her arms around him and dug her fingers into his back, pulling him closer. She was warm and soft and sweet. Holding her in his arms, kissing her, Shourya saw his entire life in her. He promised himself he would always protect her, he would do anything for her.

Words could not describe what he felt for her, how much she meant to him. But he tried. 'We will make it through this, okay? Just have some faith. I am right here with you, I will always be there with you; we are in this together.'

Lavanya nodded.

'We'll be all right,' he said.

'We'll be all right,' Lavanya repeated.

Epilogue

The first time they got married, they did it in a court. It was a formal affair. She wore a simple white dress, he wore a suit—that was the most effort they put into it. They did not care much about a celebration. All that mattered was that they were with each other, and they were in love.

They lived in California for a couple of years, working and doing random, fun things . . . *without* following a list. Their parents visited them regularly. Lavanya loved having not one, but two families. Shourya continued his job, but Lavanya did not join another high profile corporate law firm. She worked as an environmental lawyer for a non-profit organization. Her cases were not high priority, there weren't millions at stake, but she was happy, content. It was her chance to make a difference.

But now, two years later, they decided it was time to move back to India. They had paid off the bulk of their student loans, so there were no financial obligations that kept them there. In the beginning, they'd been scared and more inclined to get treatment from specialists in the US, but after two years, they were more familiar with her disease and, therefore, more confident. She was doing well. Her body was responding to the treatment. They'd met with a few hiccups along the way, but they only learned from it and got stronger. So finally, one night, at dinner, when Shourya said something about moving back to Delhi, Lavanya jumped at the chance. Just like that, it was decided.

Lavanya adjusted her veil again. She was wearing a deep red lehenga. People had told her it was out of fashion. She did not care. They wanted to do it the traditional way this time.

'Watch your step, beta,' her father said, holding her hand to help her climb down the porch steps that led to the lawn in front of their home. She squeezed his hand before letting it go.

Her mother hugged her and said, 'You look beautiful.' She guided her to the mandap where the priest and Shourya were waiting for her.

As Lavanya climbed on to the mandap, Toughy trotting at her heel, she saw Shourya's face for the first time that night. He had shaved off the French beard she had been begging him to get rid off for weeks. With his hair trimmed and his perfect smile, he looked like quite the gentleman. As if on cue, he got up to escort her to her seat, two feet away from where she was.

'Ma'am,' he offered his hand to her.

'Thank you,' she laughed. As they sat down, she whispered to him, 'You gave me peace, in a lifetime of war.'

'Oh, stop it, you, with the *Troy* reference!'

They were laughing. With him, she was always laughing. She wondered if there was anything better than being married to her best friend.

Acknowledgements

Before I begin this, I pledge not to name anyone who has not directly aided and abetted me in the making of this book and/or provided me with humour/food during the time I was working on it. Dear (the rest of) family and friends, *thank you for being awesome and a part of my life*, but unfortunately, that doesn't quite cut it. Except for Maa and Papa and Bhaiya—thank you, thank you, thank you.

David Torrone, I won't call you a brilliant reader and critic because I know you'll hate that; instead I will simply thank you for always being mean to me. Artrit Bytyçi, I could say something about how adorable and hilarious you are but what matters here is that your comments were insightful and much-valued. Niki Tulk, you are hands down my favourite Australian; thank you for putting so much time and effort into every detail of my manuscript and treating it with so much love. Ava Mailloux, for being a lunatic and my heart, and Keith Baldwin for being such a sweet person and also a clown. Laura Duarte Gómez, for having unflinching and mostly groundless faith in me.

Ritu Sirkanungo, for being a retard and supplying so much entertainment in my day-to-day life. Unintentionally, but fun nonetheless. Both Purvi Bafna and Tejal Shah have

221

provided me with food at several occasions. I might've been dead right now and this book would never have seen the light of the day without you and your culinary skills. Alka Singh and Shreya Singh too for food, and Snigdha Singh and Saket Kumar for companionship during the consumption of the fore-mentioned food.

Anish Chandy, for being my agent and the person who puts up with my inconveniently timed (because of the time difference between New York and New Delhi; I'm not an insensitive person), panicked phone calls, mostly senseless questions and all other troubles that come with having me in your life. Also, of course, for your amazing suggestions for the manuscript.

The team at Penguin Random House: Vaishali Mathur, I have so much to thank you for, you've been by my side every step of the way on my journey as a writer, not just as an editor but much, much more. Shatarupa Ghoshal, it may not be considered appropriate, but I'm going to go ahead and say it anyway—you're the best copy editor I've ever worked with. Aparajita Ninan for the beautiful cover design. And the people who come in and take over once a manuscript becomes a book—Aman Arora, Caroline Newbury and Priyanka Sabarwal.

Guruji Sri Sri Paramhansa Yogananda, for strength, for faith, for hope.

And now, in the end, I'm going to use that cheesy line where I thank *you*, the reader, for picking up this book and tell you how much I hope you like it. You rock.